BEST ENEMIES

Other books in the
CANTERWOOD CREST SERIES:

TAKE THE REINS

CHASING BLUE

BEHIND THE BIT

TRIPLE FAULT

CANTERWOOD CREST

BEST ENEMIES

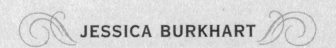

JESSICA BURKHART

ALADDIN M!X

New York London Toronto Sydney

ALADDIN M!X

Simon & Schuster Children's Publishing Division

1230 Avenue of the Americas, New York, NY 10020

First Aladdin M!X edition October 2009

Text copyright © 2009 by Jessica Burkhart

All rights reserved, including the right of reproduction
in whole or in part in any form.

ALADDIN is a trademark of Simon & Schuster, Inc., and related logo
is a registered trademark of Simon & Schuster, Inc.

ALADDIN M!X and related logo are registered trademarks
of Simon & Schuster, Inc.

For information about special discounts for bulk purchases, please
contact Simon & Schuster Special Sales at 1-866-506-1949
or business@simonandschuster.com.

The Simon & Schuster Speakers Bureau can bring authors to your live event.
For more information or to book an event contact the Simon & Schuster Speakers
Bureau at 1-866-248-3049 or visit our website at www.simonspeakers.com.

Designed by Jessica Handelman

The text of this book was set in Venetian 301 BT.

Manufactured in the United States of America

6 8 10 9 7

Library of Congress Control Number 2009929573

ISBN 978-1-4169-9037-6

ISBN 978-1-4169-9692-7 (eBook)

0212 OFF

To Twitter and HorseChick

for pulling a 007

that Bond would envy

ACKNOWLEDGMENTS

Alyssa Henkin, thank you for always being excited to read the latest adventure with Sasha & Co.

Kate Angelella—the Eric and Sasha date scene is my favorite of the series because of your sparkly note. Let's discuss.

Thanks to my friends—both online and RL—who cheered me on through this draft.

Ross, thanks for showing me your version of NYC life, which is fast becoming mine.

And, Kate, you already know, but "lifesaver" doesn't even begin to cover it. LYB!

Finally, to the fans who e-mail me photos and drawings and ask for boy advice—you're the best!

BEST ENEMIES

I

THE VERDICT

THE LEADER OF THE TRIO STOOD FROZEN IN the doorway of the Winchester common room. I never imagined I'd live to see perfect, fierce Heather Fox looking this way. Her face was pale. Her usually glossed lips were bare and her mascara smudged.

My stomach tightened. The news about Julia's and Alison's fate couldn't be good.

"Heather, what *happened*?" I asked again. "What? Tell me." I slid off the couch and stood, facing her.

She walked to the fireplace and wrapped her arms across her chest.

"Heather—" I started.

Her blue eyes were teary when she looked at me. "It's so awful," she said. "Julia and Alison. They—" Heather buried her face in her hands and, in that moment, I forgot we were enemies.

"C'mon," I said. I put my hand on her elbow and guided her toward the couch. I sat beside her, surprised when she didn't snap at me to get out of her space.

After a few seconds she sat up straighter and began to talk.

"I waited in Orchard for Julia and Alison," Heather said. "When they finally showed up, they were a mess. They were sobbing. I mean, I could barely understand them."

"Okay," I coaxed. "Then what?"

"Julia said that Headmistress Drake called their parents," Heather said. "She told them that Julia and Alison had cheated on their history exam. Alison said they told the headmistress a million times they hadn't, but Drake insisted there was proof."

Heather sighed, rubbing her temples. Whatever she was about to say, I knew it was bad.

Heather took a deep breath, turning to me. Her face was blank. "Julia and Alison got kicked off the advanced team."

2

PERMANENTLY

I TRUDGED THROUGH A LIGHT DRIZZLE ON the way to my advanced riding lesson the next morning. The dark gray clouds looked as if they'd burst into torrents at any second and all I wanted to do was turn around and climb back into bed.

Thinking about Julia and Alison had kept me awake all night. I'd gone back and forth between feeling sorry for them and being angry. If they'd really cheated then they deserved to be kicked off the team. But *did* they cheat? My gut said yes.

I ducked into the black and white stable, passing Trix's stall. The bay mare had her head stuck over the dark-lacquered stall door, probably looking for Julia.

"I'll bring you a treat later," I promised her.

I pulled open the tack room door. Rows of gleaming saddles sat along the walls and shiny bridles hung from gold hooks. The intricate, ornate details of Canterwood's gorgeous stable never got old.

Callie Harper, my on-again BFF, stepped out from around the corner. She had Black Jack's saddle and bridle in her arms. I noticed that she was wearing the new pair of brown breeches we'd picked out of the Dover catalog last week—online shopping had been just one of the many things I'd missed doing together when we'd been fighting weeks ago.

"It's going to be weird without Julia and Alison today," she said.

I nodded. "How long do you think they'll be off the team?"

Callie shrugged, shifting the saddle. "A month maybe? I saw Julia in the Orchard common room right before I came to the stable."

"What'd she say?"

"Nothing. She looked so mad—like she couldn't even talk. She just brushed right by me."

"Can you imagine? They can't even ride. I mean, what about—"

"The YENT," Callie said, finishing my sentence. "I know, I was thinking that too."

"I guess we'll find out in a few minutes."

I gathered Charm's tack and we left the room, splitting up in the aisle. The YENT—or the Youth Equestrian National Team—was the team we'd all been working toward since the beginning of the year. It was part of the most exclusive riding program in the country and only a few new riders were chosen each year. Callie, Julia, Heather, Alison, Jasmine, and I had made it through two rounds of testing for the YENT scouts. Our final test was only five weeks away.

"Hi, Charm," I said, calling to my chestnut Thoroughbred/Belgian gelding. Charm nickered to me and I reached out to rub his blaze.

I clipped a lead line onto his brown leather halter and led him out of his roomy box stall. He stood still while I attached the crossties. I hurried through grooming him, ready to get to the arena. I wanted to get through Mr. Conner's announcement and start focusing on what really mattered—the YENT.

I trotted Charm into the arena and joined Heather and Callie, who were already warming up Aristocrat and Jack along the wall. Heather's seat was stiff and

Aristocrat—Heather's Thoroughbred—jerked his head up and down, seesawing the reins against his neck. Mr. Conner, our riding instructor, walked into the center of the arena.

"Please line up in front of me," he called.

Jack and Charm flanked Aristocrat as we all came to a stop in front of Mr. Conner. He folded his arms and his six-foot frame made him look intimidating, even from my spot on horseback. "By now, I'm sure you're all aware that Julia and Alison will not be joining us," Mr. Conner said. "They have been removed from the advanced team. Permanently."

Beside me, Callie gasped. *Permanently*. Not a month. Not until fall. But permanently.

Beside me, Heather backed Aristocrat out from between Jack and Charm. She looked at Mr. Conner, her face red. "I have to—excuse me," she mumbled.

Mr. Conner only nodded and watched as Heather spun Aristocrat away from us and trotted him out of the arena.

Um, wow. No one had *ever* walked out on a lesson before. But Mr. Conner must have understood how hard this was for Heather—Julia and Alison were her best friends.

"Cheating is not tolerated by Canterwood Crest

Academy," Mr. Conner continued. "And it's certainly not acceptable behavior for riders on any of my teams. Julia and Alison will not be riding until next January. When they do resume lessons, they'll be joining the intermediate team. From there, they'll have to prove that they're ready to join the advanced team again."

"But what about the YENT?" Callie asked, her eyes wide. "Tryouts."

Mr. Conner shook his head. "They are no longer part of the advanced team, so they will not be riding for scouts."

Charm snorted and stepped back. I looked down and realized I'd pulled on the reins. "Sorry," I whispered.

Mr. Conner would never change his mind. Julia and Alison's YENT dreams were officially over for the year. I couldn't even imagine how they must have felt finding that out.

"Since there are now two fewer riders on the advanced team," Mr. Conner said. "I'll be testing two promising intermediate riders within the next couple of weeks. If their tests are successful, they will join the advanced team."

Eric and Jasmine—it had to be. Eric's riding improved with every passing week and if Jasmine hadn't been so forceful with Phoenix during the last test, she would have already made the team.

"I know this is upsetting news," Mr. Conner said. "But the best thing for us to do is just get back to work. So move your horses out to the wall and do a sitting trot."

For the next half hour, I went through the motions of the lesson. Charm did his best—like always—but my mind was on Julia and Alison. One stupid mistake had cost them everything.

After class, I handed Charm to Mike—my favorite groom who took care of Charm after morning lessons—and headed out of the stable. On my way out of the stable, my phone buzzed.

Guess what?

Eric—my boyfriend. I grinned when I thought the b-word to myself. It was still totally new to me.

What?

Mr. C wants 2 test me 4 adv team.

I KNEW IT!!! :) Tell me mr ltr!

I pocketed my phone, smiling as I walked. There were so many positive things to think about. My boyfriend was going to make the advanced team—I knew he would. After all Callie and I had gone through, we were BFFs again. Jasmine, even though she was still a threat, was at least on Heather's radar and I knew that Heather could deal with it. Charm and I were going to practice nonstop for the YENT. My smile faltered when I thought about Julia and Alison.

But they had made their choices, I reminded myself—I had to stay focused on mine.

3

TABLE FOR TWO

I SLID INTO MY TABLE AT THE NOISY CAF AND
Eric took the seat across from me. A table for two. We'd
finally gone public on Monday after I'd told Callie and
Jacob that I was with Eric. Our open BF/GF status still felt
a little weird after keeping it under wraps for so long.

"Feels strange without Paige chaperoning, huh?" Eric
asked, reading my mind.

I laughed. "My thoughts exactly."

Paige Parker, my other BFF and roommate, had covered
for Eric and me for weeks. I'd kept Eric a secret because
I'd been afraid of losing him like I'd lost Jacob—my
ex–almost-boyfriend. Heather had almost broken us up,
but it had ultimately been Callie who finished the job.
She hadn't meant to, but while things between me and

Jacob were at their rockiest, Callie had fallen for him. It had taken weeks for Callie and me to work through it, but now we'd moved on.

Callie was happy with Jacob. I was crazy about Eric. Happily ever blah, blah, blah.

I took a bite of my grilled cheese and looked across the caf. Jasmine was sitting with Violet, Brianna, and Georgia—riders on the eighth-grade advanced team who called themselves the Belles. No one walked too close to that table. Not unless you were one of *them*. The three girls threw back their heads in laughter at something pretty, dark-haired Jasmine had just said.

I looked away from them, glancing at Eric. *Snap out of it,* I told myself.

"So, did Mr. Conner give you a testing date yet?" I asked.

"Not yet," Eric said. "But I hope I'm ready."

I reached across the table and touched his hand. "You're ready. And weirdly calm, by the way."

"It's all an act," Eric said, laughing. "I'm actually kind of freaking out."

I smiled. "It's too bad you can't ride for the YENT scouts too," I said. Eric hadn't already ridden twice in front of the scouts to qualify for the June YENT trials.

"I guess. But to be honest, I want to spend some time on the advanced team first—if I make it. I've got a long way to go before I'd even be ready for YENT tryouts."

I shook my head. "No way. You're the best jumper at Canterwood. They'd be lucky to have you."

"You're biased," Eric said with a laugh, popping a French fry into his mouth. "And this is *your* time. You're going to be the seventh-grade star who makes the YENT. I'm telling you—I can feel it."

At that moment I just wanted to kiss him. But people were eating and that would be gross, right? I settled for smiling.

"So . . . tomorrow," I said. "You do remember what tomorrow is, right?"

"Tomorrow?" Eric drummed his fingers on the table. "Hmm. Nope. Can't think of anything going on tomorrow."

"Eric!" I kicked him under the table. "You remember."

He gave me a blank stare for a couple of seconds before smiling. "Ohhh, *tomorrow*. Yeah, now that you mentioned it. I'm going on my first official date with my girlfriend what's-her-name. Remind her if you see her, okay?"

I rolled my eyes. "Well, whoever she is, I bet she's superexcited."

And nervous. And thrilled. And probably won't-be-sleeping-at-all-tonight.

Heels clicked on the floor and I looked up to see Heather. She didn't look as pale as yesterday, but I could still see the stress on her face—even concealer couldn't hide her dark circles. She gave me a half smile and nodded at Eric.

"Finally, Silver," she said, walking off before I could say anything.

Heather had guessed my secret at Paige's *Teen Cuisine* premiere party on Friday. She'd encouraged—and by "encouraged," I mean "threatened"—me to tell Callie about Eric so I could finally be open about our relationship. The party, meant to spotlight Paige's new gig as the host of a show on The Food Network for Kids, hadn't gone at all like I'd planned.

Eric looked at me sideways.

"She actually gave me good advice once," I said. "Not that I *ever* admitted that."

"Admitted what?"

Eric and I finished eating and agreed to text each other later. I was hurrying down the hallway, shuffling through songs on my iPod, when I looked up to see Julia and Alison.

"Stop looking at us like that," Julia said.

"Like what?" I asked.

Julia tucked a lock of her blond bob behind her ear. "Like we're losers who cheat."

I shrugged. "Not that I was looking at you in *any* way. But you did cheat."

Alison's cheeks went pink. "We. Did. Not. Cheat!"

"You never studied," I said. "Every time we were at the library, I saw you messing around instead of studying."

"So we didn't study at the library. So what? You don't live at Orchard—you wouldn't have seen the work we did there," Julia argued. "And why would we cheat this close to the YENT? We'd *never* mess with that."

It was just too difficult to believe her. Canterwood classes were beyond hard—no one knew that more than me. If they hadn't studied enough, it wouldn't have taken a big leap to believe they'd cheated. And the headmistress had said there'd been proof—so what were we even arguing about?

Julia stepped closer to me when a group of girls walked by us. "You know what? I wouldn't have cared what anyone thought—but they took riding away from us for something we didn't do."

I sighed. "But if you didn't—"

"We *didn't*," Alison interrupted.

"Then prove it," I said, walking away.

4

KEYWORD: EMERGENCY

WHEN I GOT TO WINCHESTER LATER THAT afternoon, I dropped my heavy book bag on the floor of our dorm room and went straight to my closet. Paige wasn't back yet, which was very unfortunate because this was prime BFF/roommate bonding material. I pulled open the doors and started yanking out every possible date outfit. Why was everything I owned suddenly so pathetic and horrible? I tugged every shirt off its hanger, took out all of my shoes, and went through every skirt in my closet. Nothing screamed *first date*.

The only thing I was sure that I'd wear was my charm bracelet. Not exactly an outfit.

The dorm room door opened. Paige stopped and put her hands on her hips as she surveyed the mess. Clothes were piled on my purple bedspread, over our tiny coffee table, and on my desk.

"Um," she said, closing the door.

"Paige!" I wailed. "All of this is wrong. Help!"

Holding back a laugh, Paige pulled her red hair into a ponytail and picked up clothes as she walked across the room. "Turn on your laptop," she said. "You have to feel confident. If none of these clothes work, we'll find you something that does."

"And that's why you're my favorite roommate," I said.

"I'm your *only* roommate," Paige pointed out.

She helped me hang up my clothes while the computer started. We put it on the center of my bed and sat cross-legged in front of it.

Paige took over the mouse. "Definitely a blue shirt," she said. "You look good in blue."

She clicked through Express's website and with expertise that only comes from being a Manhattan shopper, she quickly selected a floaty knee-length black skirt, black kitten heels, and a baby-blue top with three-quarter sleeves.

"Like?" she asked as we reviewed the items in my cart.

"Love," I said. "You totally saved my date."

Paige nodded. "Obviously. Since Eric only likes you for your clothes."

I hopped off the bed and grabbed my "emergencies only" credit card from my desk drawer.

"My date's tomorrow," I said. "Overnight shipping is the only option or the clothes won't be here in time. This qualifies as emergency, right?"

Paige nodded. "Duh."

I clicked the order button and crossed my fingers that Mom and Dad would agree on the emergency status. I shut off my laptop and walked to the door.

"I owe you popcorn and soda," I said. "Be right back."

"'Kay," Paige said. She barely looked up from rearranging the clothes she'd hung back up in my closet. That was my Paige.

In the common room I grabbed a bag of kettle corn and popped it into the microwave. Popcorn was pretty much the only thing Paige trusted me to make. I'd only ruined it once when I'd hit twenty-two minutes instead of two, left the common room, and forgotten to come back. Luckily, Livvie—our dorm monitor—had noticed my mistake before the bag caught fire. But the entire dorm had smelled like burned popcorn for weeks.

I waited for the popcorn and looked up when the door opened. Jasmine stepped inside, looking like *she* was going on a date tonight in an off-the-shoulder black shirt and vintage-looking jeans. She stared at me.

"What?" I asked.

"Oh, just got an e-mail from Mr. Conner," she said, grabbing a ginger ale from the fridge. "Eric and I are testing next week. On Sunday."

"Good luck," I said. "I know Eric's going to be practicing nonstop."

Jas hopped onto the counter and looked at me. "What's it like going out with Intermediate Eric?"

"Stop calling him that," I said. "'Cuz then I have to keep reminding you that you're intermediate too."

"Till next week," Jas said. "But your boyfriend doesn't belong on the advanced team and you know it."

The microwave timer beeped. "Whatever," I said. "We'll see who makes it and who doesn't."

I turned away from her, opened the microwave, and retrieved my popcorn. I poured it into a bowl and headed out of the room.

"You're the one who needs luck," Jasmine called. "You're totally delusional about your chances at the YENT."

I slammed the door behind me before she could say another word.

She was wrong. My chances were as good as anyone's— and I was going to make sure it stayed that way.

5

AQUAPHOBIA

ON FRIDAY AFTERNOON I WAS IN MY FAVORITE place in the world—Charm's saddle. The April air was warm and the sun beamed down on Callie, Heather, and me. The recent rain had made the grass lush and I knew Charm was eyeing every clump of clover. Mr. Conner had taken us to the outdoor cross-country course—my and Charm's favorite.

Mr. Conner gathered us around him. "We're going to do the modified version of the course," he said. "Take your horse over the path you walked yesterday. I'll be waiting at the other side of the woods. Heather will go first. Sasha, count to one hundred before you start." I nodded. "Callie, please do the same after Sasha."

Heather, Callie, and I traded smiles. Today was going

to be fun! Mr. Conner hadn't brought up Heather skipping out on the last lesson and she had shown up today with her game face on.

"I'm going to take a shortcut to the other side. Remember that if something happens, another rider will be just behind you. Callie, if we don't see you a couple of minutes after Sasha finishes, I'll find you on the course, okay?"

"Okay," Callie said.

"Heather, you may go when you're ready," Mr. Conner said. He started across the field.

Heather turned Aristocrat toward the course, then looked over at me. "Oh, don't look so smug, Silver," she said, rolling her eyes. "You're not the only one who can do cross-country."

Callie and I made *well, excuse me* faces at Heather behind her back when she turned around. She pushed her black helmet down on her head and settled into the saddle. She heeled Aristocrat forward and the dark chestnut leaped into a collected canter.

Heather's gold-blond hair streamed out behind her as Aristocrat's hooves churned up the grass and they darted away. Aristocrat jumped the low stone wall and they disappeared into the woods.

"She's good," I said. "Unfortunately."

Callie nodded. "Very unfortunate."

I brushed a blade of grass off the sleeve of my plum-colored jacket. "You getting nervous about the YENT?" I asked.

"Yeah," Callie said. "But we still have, what, five weeks? We can practice all the time."

"Totally," I said. "We'll be ready."

Relief washed over me that we were friends again. I'd missed her more than I'd even realized.

"Okay," Callie said. "You can probably go now."

"Wish me luck!" I tensed in the saddle, shoving down my heels and adjusting my grip on Charm's reins. I'd picked the ones with rubber grips for today.

"Gooo, Sasha!" Callie cheered, doing an awkward dance in the saddle.

I tossed a grin over my shoulder at her as I urged Charm into a trot. Three strides later, he broke into a canter and I focused on the stone wall.

At the just the right moment he lifted into the air and I gripped with my knees to stay in the saddle. He landed easily on the other side and we cantered the last few yards of open field as the course shifted into the woods. I slowed Charm as my eyes adjusted to the darker lighting.

The trees cast strange shadows over the woods and a light wind blew through the leaves.

We cantered a few more strides before we approached a three-foot log pile. *Three, two, and up!* I chanted in my head. Charm snapped his knees beneath him and lifted into the air. He cleared the logs with ease, pointing his ears forward when we landed—his attention drifting.

"Hey, pay attention," I said, doing a half halt. Charm, listening, flicked both ears back to me.

We cantered down the dirt path that twisted through the woods. Charm leaped a few fallen trees that had been laid purposely across our path. The woods got more dense and I slowed him to a fast trot. Uh-oh. We were about to approach the creek.

At this part of the course we were supposed to trot down the creek's bank, splash through the water and climb up the other side. But last week, Charm had developed a random creek phobia. He wanted to try and leap the span of the creek to avoid the water. But most sections were too wide for that.

I leaned back in the saddle as we started down the incline. I tightened my knees on the saddle and focused on not tipping forward over Charm's neck. Charm's ears flicked back and forth as we approached the creek. Clear water rushed over the creek bed and a few pebbles sparkled as sunlight peeked through the canopy of trees.

"C'mon," I said. "You've got it, boy."

But Charm's stride slowed with every step. He leaned back, digging his heels into the soft dirt before the creek. I gritted my teeth, urging him forward with my hands and seat, but he sidestepped instead of going forward.

I pressed my boot heels against his sides and sat deep in the saddle. Beneath me, Charm fought my hands and legs—intent on not getting in the water. I turned him away from the creek and, snorting with relief, he started to scramble back up the bank. But I pulled hard on the left rein, turning him back toward the water.

"Charm, come on," I said, squeezing my legs tighter against his sides. He sidestepped again, his front hooves just inches from the water. For a second, I thought he was going to rock back on his haunches and try to jump, but the creek was too wide. Charm stood, trembling, and I did the worst thing possible: I gave up.

I sat back in the saddle and relaxed my exhausted arms and legs. I moved Charm to the side of the creek and off the course.

"You can't keep doing this," I said. "You *have* to go in the water. I know you hate it all of the sudden, and I'm sorry, but we'll be disqualified if you pull this in competition. You used to *love* water."

Charm flicked an ear back at my voice and lowered his head. I looked up when I heard hoofbeats in the woods. Jack trotted down the path and Callie's eyes flickered in my direction.

"What happened?" she asked, urging Jack over to Charm and me.

I shook my head. "Charm won't go through the creek. Can we follow you across?"

"Sure thing," Callie said. "Let's start from back there." She pointed a gloved hand toward the top of the gentle slope.

We guided Charm and Jack away from the creek. Charm seemed calmed by Jack's presence.

"I wish he hadn't suddenly developed this weird water problem *now*," I said. "Not so close to the YENT."

Callie looked over and locked eyes with me. "Don't worry. We'll fix it," she promised. "I'll help."

"Thanks, Callie." We turned the horses to face the creek.

"I'll go first," Callie said. "Keep Charm behind us. He'll follow Jack right over."

I nodded, gripping the reins tighter.

Callie trotted Jack forward and I started Charm behind him. Charm, eager to stay with Jack, followed him down the bank without hesitation.

"Keep him moving," Callie called over her shoulder.

"Got it!" I said.

Jack stepped into the creek, water splashing over his royal blue leg wraps. He trotted quickly through the creek. Charm, hesitating, looked at Jack and started to weave at the creek's edge.

"No, *go*," I said, keeping my voice firm and low.

Charm shuddered, then leaped into the water. He took bounding strides forward and I almost lost my stirrups—his long stride caught me off guard. He followed Jack out of the creek and the horses climbed the bank, stepping in hoof prints that had to be Aristocrat's.

"He did it!" Callie cheered. We pulled the horses side by side.

I shook my head. "But did you see *how* he did it? And I wouldn't have even gotten him over if you hadn't been here with Jack."

"Sash, it happens. You have time to work with him before the YENT. I'll come out here with you whenever you want to practice and I know Eric will too."

I gave her a small smile. "You're right. I know you're right."

"Let's finish this," Callie said. "We should just stick together now. Mr. Conner will understand."

I waved my hand in a you-go-ahead gesture. "We'll follow you."

Callie urged Jack into a canter and Charm and I shot off after them. We finished the rest of the course within minutes.

Back at the stable Callie and I cooled Jack and Charm and crosstied them next to each other. I'd missed hanging out with her at the stable. Callie was my fave person to share horsey gossip with.

"And you told them *what*?" Callie asked, giggling.

"Just that Eric had a girlfriend and they were happy together," I said.

Callie's shoulders shook with laughter. "They had no clue *you* were the girlfriend?"

"Nope," I said. "None."

I'd just told Callie about the beginner and intermediate riders I'd heard a few weeks ago talking about the gorgeous new guy on their riding team. A guy they all wanted, especially one girl—Rachel. I'd thought the conversation was cute and funny until they said *Eric's* name. I wanted to burst into the room and tell them he was taken, but our relationship had been a secret then.

"When they see you with him," Callie said, "it'll be awesome."

"Totally."

We laughed and both looked up when we heard hoofbeats. Eric stopped Luna in front of us.

"Getting ready for a lesson?" I asked.

"I hope you wore Mr. Conner down a little before I go in."

"No way," Callie said. "He'll be turning up the pressure on your group—especially since you and Jas are testing."

"I'm kind of jealous that you get to test in a week," I said. "Callie and I have to wait forever."

Eric nodded. "But you'll have more time to practice." Eric looked as if he wanted to say something else, but stopped short. His warm gaze changed to a stony glare.

I turned and saw Jacob walking down the aisle toward us, careful not to get too close to any of the horses.

"Hey," Callie said when she saw him. "What are you doing here?"

Jacob, keeping a safe distance from Charm, Luna, and Jack, shoved his hands into the pockets of his jeans.

"Thought I'd pick you up and see if you were up for a trip to the Sweet Shoppe."

"Sounds good," Callie said. "I'm done here. Let me just put Jack back in his stall."

Callie unclipped the crossties and led Jack down the aisle. Jacob looked after her, but stayed where he was. A couple of students had the aisle blocked with horses and Jacob would have to get within inches of one to follow Callie. I wished horses didn't scare him so much.

"So," I said, trying to fill the awkward silence.

"So," Jacob said.

"I hear they have really yummy new lemon poppyseed cake at the Sweet Shoppe," I said lamely.

"Yeah?" Jacob smiled.

Eric let Luna stretch her neck toward Jacob. Jacob swallowed but didn't move.

"So," Jacob said. "What are you up to this weekend?"

"Well," I started, trying to suppress my giddy expression. "Eric and I are going to the movies tomorrow."

"On our first official date," Eric finished for me.

Jacob's green eyes flickered to me before settling on Eric. "Yeah? What a coincidence. I'm taking Callie too. We'll probably see *two* movies."

Eric shrugged. "Wow, two movies. That keeps you

from having to, I don't know, talk at all, right?"

"Guys . . . ," I started.

"Whatever, man. I hope you at least pay for Sasha's ticket. I *always* pay for Callie."

Before Eric could respond, Callie walked over and stood by Jacob.

"Ready?" she asked, her eyes darting between Jacob and me.

Jacob nodded. "Let's go."

"See you at film class," I said to Jacob, thinking that maybe if I stayed calm and friendly, it would make things less weird.

But he just gave me a quick nod.

"Text you later," Callie said.

When Jacob and Callie disappeared down the aisle, I stepped closer to Eric. "You don't have to be mad at Jacob," I said. "You know I don't like him anymore."

"I know, but I'll never be friends with that guy," Eric said. "Not after the way he treated you."

I reached out and squeezed Eric's hand. It was strong and warm, enveloping my own. Even though I hated when Eric and Jacob fought, I had to admit—it felt nice to have someone feeling protective of me.

6

OH YEAH,
NOT WEIRD AT ALL

I HURRIED DOWN THE RED-CARPETED AISLE in the theater and placed my paper on Mr. Ramirez's desk. Then I sat in my assigned seat next to Jacob. Film was one of my favorite classes, but it was weird now that Jacob and I weren't together. At least the semester was almost over.

Jacob sat next to me. He leaned forward in his seat and rifled through his backpack, then sat back up and looked straight ahead. But the next thing I knew, he was back in the bag and shuffling through papers.

"Everything . . . okay?" I asked.

"Fine." Jacob looked at me, his shaggy, sandy brown hair falling over one eye. "Why?"

"Just wondering."

He shifted in his seat and kicked over his book bag.

A black notebook slid out of the bag toward my feet. I leaned down and picked it up, holding it out to him.

"Thanks," he muttered, not looking at me.

Okaaay.

"Jacob, are you *mad* at me?" I asked.

He turned, looking me in the eyes for the first time since the stable. "No," he said. "Sorry. Just . . . something going on with a friend."

I played with the cap on my pen. "Oh. Okay. 'Cause things don't have to be weird between us. Callie and I are friends again. If you and Eric could just not do . . . *that*, then things would be easier."

Jacob just sat there. That was one thing he and Eric would agree on—they'd never be friends. I knew why Eric held a grudge against Jacob. But what was Jacob's deal?

Not knowing what else to do, I shuffled through my lip gloss bag and finally settled on a bubblegum-flavored gloss with a high shine-factor. Mr. Ramirez, frowning, was still pressing buttons on the projector.

"So . . . ," Jacob said a couple of minutes later. "Doing anything tonight?"

"Just watching *Teen Cuisine* with Paige. A new episode airs tonight."

Jacob nodded—his shoulders relaxing a little. We

started talking about *Teen Cuisine* and soon, Jacob was laughing at a story Paige had told me about the director's hideous pink and green polka dotted tie. I crossed my fingers that things would keep getting better between us.

When I got back to my room, my phone rang.

"Guess what I overheard?" Callie asked the second I answered.

"Tell me!" I dropped my bag on the floor and sat at the edge of my bed.

"I forgot my notebook in the tack room, so I went back to get it a few minutes ago," Callie said. "When I was leaving I saw Heather go into Mr. Conner's office."

"And?"

"She was pretty upset. She told Mr. Conner that Julia and Alison hadn't cheated and she didn't know what happened, but she knew they'd never do that."

I flopped backward. "What did he say?"

"That Heather was a good friend to defend them, but that Headmistress Drake *did* have proof—cheat sheets. He said he was sorry, but he wasn't going to let them back on the team."

"Heather's not going to give up," I said. "They're her friends and she believes them. It's what friends do."

7

DATE NIGHT

I WAS UP SO EARLY ON SATURDAY MORNING, cartoons weren't even on yet. Tonight was my date with Eric! I pulled on a pair of yoga pants and a jacket, trying not to wake Paige as I got dressed and flew out the door. In the cafeteria, I surveyed my food options. First date day deserved a special breakfast. I grabbed two blueberry waffles and a glass of OJ. I looked around. I definitely had my pick of tables—the caf was deserted.

I picked through my food, my thoughts focused on tonight. The idea of sitting in the darkened theater with Eric made my heart pound. The only boy I'd ever sat with at the movies had been Jacob during film class, but that had been totally different. Was I supposed to hold Eric's hand for the entire movie? My hand might get sweaty.

Then Eric would be grossed out and he'd never want to do it again.

I swallowed and pushed away my waffles. I had to ask Paige about the hand-holding sitch. I checked the time on my phone. Still early. I took small sips of my orange juice and watched as the Crush Girls—the riders I'd caught talking about Eric—came into the caf. The six girls loaded their trays with food and scanned the room, looking for empty seats. They spotted me and started whispering.

Uh-oh.

They walked up to my table and stopped.

"Can we sit?" asked Rachel, a girl on the intermediate team.

"Sure," I said.

The girls put down their trays and stared at me, not one of them touching their food.

"So . . . ," said a girl with braces. "Remember when you told us Eric Rodriguez had a girlfriend?"

"Yeaaah," I said.

"Funny," the girl said. "You never mentioned her name."

I picked up my fork and started playing with my waffles, desperate for something to do. "Well, I didn't just because I—"

"Because you *are* the girlfriend?" Rachel interrupted. She adjusted her black plastic–rimmed glasses. Artsy.

"Um." I swallowed.

"You could have just told us," said a girl with blond highlights sitting next to Rachel. "We're, like, so sorry that we were talking about your boyfriend."

"Even if he *is* gorgeous," Rachel added with a grin. She was pretty in that girl-next-door way. She was freckled and petite with a perfect, slightly upturned nose and her light brown hair had warm reddish highlights and side-swept bangs.

I smiled back. "No worries."

"Cool. But, uh, keep an eye on him," Rachel said with a wink. "*All* the girls think he's hot."

"He is," I said. "Lucky me." I picked up my tray and walked away, leaving them staring enviously after me.

For the rest of the morning and afternoon, I forced my-self to do homework. With finals only weeks away the workload was getting heavier every day. But it was no use; I couldn't concentrate on *anything*. All I could think about was tonight.

"What if he wants to see that zombie movie?" I asked Paige.

She turned away from her desk to look at me. She'd been doing homework all day too, stopping only every five minutes to answer my date questions.

"Then you go," Paige said. "Scary movies are *perfect* because every time something terrifying happens, you can bury your face in his arm. He'll love it."

"Oooh, yeah," I said. "Good point."

Paige looked at our wall clock. "It's five thirty," she said. "We either pretend to keep doing homework or start getting you ready."

My history book was closed before she'd finished her sentence. "I'm going on a date!" I said, my voice rising with every word. "Omigod! What should I do first?"

Paige grabbed my arm and pulled me off my desk chair. She pushed me gently into the bathroom and started to close the door.

"You're going to do this crazy thing called *showering*," Paige said. "Then, I'm going to do your hair. Okay?"

"Okay," I said, taking a deep breath. Paige shut the door and I hopped into the shower. I used three times the usual amount of strawberry-vanilla scented body wash before getting out. I pulled on my fluffy pink robe that Mom had given me for Christmas and let Paige blow out my hair until it was smooth and shiny.

"Get dressed and then I'll finish it off with a flatiron," she said.

I put on the clothes we'd ordered from Express, twirling in front of the mirror.

"Am I good or what?" Paige said, eyeing my outfit. "I *knew* a blue ruffle top would be perfect. And that skirt looks amazing on you!"

"It does? Are you sure?" I smoothed the skirt and peered down at it.

"Totally," Paige said. "It's first-date perfect."

I sat in the center of our room on Paige's desk chair as she straightened my hair. I fastened my charm bracelet around my wrist and put on a pair of Paige's silver chandelier earrings while she worked her flatiron magic.

Tap-tap-tap!

"Expecting company?" Paige asked, putting down the flatiron.

"Nope."

Paige opened the door.

"Hey, first-date girl," Callie said. "Can I come in?"

I waved her inside. "C'mon."

Callie came over and stood beside me, checking out my clothes. "Awesome," she said. "You look gorgeous."

"So do you!" And she did. Her dark hair hung in

loose waves around her shoulders. She'd dusted shimmery sand-colored eye shadow over her eyelids and had peachy blush on her cheeks. She wore a white one-shoulder shirt that set off her pretty caramel-brown skin, and had paired it with a light brown skirt. Callie put her purse on my bed.

"I'm glad you're here," Paige said to Callie. "You can help me do Sasha's makeup."

Callie squealed. She stepped over to the makeup counter (read: Paige's desk) and picked up the moisturizer.

Paige spun me away from the mirror. "We're *so* not letting Sasha peek until we're done."

"Agreed." Callie started to put a dab of moisturizer on my cheek.

"Wait!" Paige yelled.

"What? What's wrong?" Callie jumped back, yanking her hand away from my face.

Paige giggled. "Sorry. You have to pick a makeup artist name. It's, like, our tradition. I'm always Jade and Sasha is Kiki."

Callie thought for a second. "Gisele."

"Good one!" I said, high-fiving her.

I settled back into the chair and let Jade and Gisele get to work. Getting my makeup done was relaxing and it kept me from worrying about my date.

Twenty minutes later Paige and Callie stepped back to look at me.

"We're going to spin you around," Paige said slowly.

They turned my chair toward the full-length mirror in our room. I blinked at my reflection.

"Wow," I said softly. "You guys are good."

Paige and Callie smiled behind me.

Tinted moisturizer had evened out my skin tone. A shimmery dusting of barely-there blush highlighted my cheekbones. My eyelashes were darkened with a coat of mascara and Paige had lined my eyes with a smoky, light gray liner that made my green eyes appear even greener.

"Um, but no lip gloss," I said.

"Oh, yeah," Callie said, turning to Paige's desk and rummaging through the lip gloss container. "I really don't think any of these will work."

I stood and looked into the box. "What? None of these? Why?" There were at least twenty to choose from. One *had* to work. "Look in my bag."

But Callie reached into her purse and pulled out a small package wrapped with sparkly pink paper. "I think you should use *this* instead."

"Callie!" I took the gift from her and tore open the

wrapping. Under the pretty paper was a Stila Lip Glaze in papaya. "Omigod, it's perfect!"

I hugged her, keeping one eye on the lip gloss at all times.

"I'm so glad you like it," Callie said. "You totally needed a first date gloss. I spent hours on the site to pick the perfect shade."

I twisted open the lip gloss pen and carefully applied a coat of the sheer soft pink.

"That's exactly what you needed," Paige said. "You're ready now."

I swallowed, rubbing my palms together. "I'm sweaty!" I said. "My hands are slick and Eric's going to think——"

"That you like him enough to be nervous," Callie said, cutting me off. "It's okay to be nervous. It's your first date. But it's *Eric*. You know him and you really like him. It's going to be great."

Paige moved to stand next to Callie. "It will be *amazing*," Paige confirmed.

"Okay," I said, taking a deep breath. "I can do this."

"Have fun," Callie said. I hugged her, then Paige. They made me feel confident. I could *so* do this. I slipped on my black cropped cardi-wrap sweater and stepped out into the hallway.

On my way out, I stopped in the doorway of Livvie's office. "I'll be back in a couple of hours, okay?" I asked her. I'd already cleared tonight with her, but I wanted to double check.

She nodded. "Have fun, Sash."

Eric was meeting me right outside. He'd wanted to come inside to pick me up at my room, but I hadn't wanted to push it with Livvie. She'd already let Eric inside Winchester once. Before I pushed open the door, I took a breath. *It's just Eric,* I reminded myself. And that made me smile.

8

CHICK FLICKS AND
THE GUYS WHO
LOVE THEM

WHEN I OPENED THE DOOR I FELT LIKE I WAS
on a movie set. Eric was leaning against the black railing, looking perfect in a long-sleeve black shirt and dark wash jeans. Behind Eric the sky, now a dark purple, was twinkling with early stars.

"You look beautiful," he said. "Wow."

My anxiety melted the second I heard his voice. "Thanks. You look great too."

Eric clasped my hand in his and we walked down the steps.

"Oh," Eric said. "Wait a sec." He stopped and let go of my hand. He reached into his back pocket and pulled out a small blue box. He held it out to me. "This is for you."

I took the box, my fingers shaking a little. "Eric, you didn't have to get me anything."

He shook his head. "It's our first date, Sasha. I want it to be special."

I untied a skinny white ribbon and lifted the lid of the box. Inside, a tiny silver horseshoe charm was nestled on a piece of cotton.

"Eric," I gasped. "It's gorgeous!" I touched the cool surface of the charm.

His brown eyes warmed as he looked at me. "I hoped you'd like it. I never see you without your bracelet, so I wanted to get you something for it. Paige helped."

"I love it." I held out my wrist to Eric. "Will you put it on?"

He picked up the charm and fastened it to my bracelet. I shivered when his fingers brushed the inside of my wrist. The horseshoe fit so well with the horse charm my parents had given me.

"It's beautiful," I said. "I'm going to look at it whenever I need luck, which will only be every five seconds."

He laughed as I stuck the box in my purse.

"You don't need luck," Eric said, taking my hand again. "But now you've got it just in case."

As we started walking, I couldn't help but think that

I'd been nervous over nothing. It was Eric. My *boyfriend* Eric—and we were going to have fun tonight.

When we reached the media center, we wandered through the giant lobby and got in line. The Friday night line was almost out the door. At the Canterwood movie theater, tickets and concessions were sold in the same line.

"I'm thinking we need lots of popcorn with tons of butter and a mix of sweet and sour candy," I said. "You agree?"

"Like Junior Mints, AirHeads, Nerds, and Twizzlers?" Eric asked.

"And that's why you're my boyfriend."

The line moved forward and we inched ahead.

"Sasha, hey."

I turned and saw Callie. With Jacob. They were in the line beside us.

"Hi," I said to both of them. "You guys here for a movie?"

Duh, I thought before Callie or Jacob even responded.

"Yeah," Callie said, slipping her fingers through Jacob's.

I tucked my hair behind my ear and caught Jacob staring at my wrist. He looked away when he saw me watching him. Callie followed Jacob's gaze, her eyes widening when she saw my bracelet. Our eyes met and I held my wrist out to her. "Eric gave me a new charm."

"Oooh!" Callie squealed. "I love it! That was so sweet."

I glanced at Eric. "I know. I'm totally spoiled. Lip gloss from you and a charm from Eric."

Jacob shifted and looked away. Callie and I traded glances, but didn't say anything. We knew it was useless to try and make them be cool with each other.

It was Eric's turn at the counter, so he stepped up to order.

"Hi," he said. "Two tickets for *Zoe's Guide to Getting the Guy*. And I'll take a large popcorn, one medium Diet Coke and one medium Dr Pepper—"

I smiled when he knew my favorite soda was Diet Coke and listened as he ordered enough candy to give us a sugar high for a week.

While Eric waited for his change, it was Jacob's turn to order. "I need an *extra* large popcorn, two large Sprites, some king size Skittles, a Hershey's bar, two boxes of Lemonheads, a box of—"

"Hey," Callie said gently, interrupting him. "Are you bringing a second girlfriend on this date? That's plenty of stuff—really."

Jacob turned back to the cashier. "That's it."

"Forget something?" Eric asked Jacob.

Jacob glared at Eric. "What?"

Eric hid a smirk. "Tickets, maybe?"

Jacob's tan face turned a deep red.

"I've got it," Callie said in a light tone. "Two tickets for *Revenge of the Killer Zombies*, please."

"Wait," Jacob said. He leaned forward toward the cashier. "She means tickets for *Zoe's Guide to Getting the Guy*."

What?

"We don't want to see that," Callie said. "It's supposed to be a super–girly-romantic movie. You'll hate it."

"We have to see it," Jacob said, blushing. "Uh, Mr. Ramirez wants us to watch all different kinds of movies. Including ones we normally wouldn't like."

True. But film class was almost over. Jacob was doing this just to bug me. He wanted to tag along on my date with Eric to have a chance to prove the entire time that he was the better boyfriend.

The cashier handed him the tickets and Jacob loaded his arms with the candy and popcorn. Callie grabbed the sodas.

Jacob practically stomped off toward the theater.

Eric and I followed Callie and Jacob into the dimly lit hallway and we made our way down the aisle, looking for empty seats. Callie and Jacob slid into a row in the back.

I walked until Eric and I were halfway down the theater. "This okay?" I asked.

Eric nodded. "Perfect." We found two seats and I smoothed my skirt when I sat down. I tried not to think about the fact that my ex–almost-boyfriend was behind me. I wanted to enjoy my date.

Eric put the popcorn bucket between us and we put our drinks in the cup holders. The lights dimmed and the movie started. *This was it!*

I reached into the popcorn bucket at the same time Eric did. Our fingers brushed together and I blushed, glad it was dark in the theater. We'd held hands a zillion times, but tonight felt different. I'd almost jerked my hand out of the bucket when he'd touched me.

I took a handful of popcorn and started munching. Eric passed the Twizzlers to me and I broke off a piece before handing it back to him.

We watched a few more minutes of the movie, but I wanted to talk to him. "You going riding tomorrow?" I whispered.

"Yeah. Lesson. But I really want to trail ride. I—"

"Shhhh!" someone said behind us.

"Sorry!" Eric and I whispered simultaneously. I tipped

watermelon Nerds into my mouth and tried to concentrate on the movie, but I couldn't. Sitting here and not saying anything was torture! We finished the popcorn and Eric moved the bucket to the empty seat beside him so he could hold my hand over the armrest.

My hand felt warm and tingly as he held it.

I looked over at him and we traded a glance—I knew he was thinking the same thing I was.

"Want to get out of here?" he whispered.

"Yes!"

We grabbed our stuff, ducking as we tiptoed down the row and out into the aisle.

We passed Callie and Jacob. I gave Callie a thumbs up to let her know nothing was wrong. Callie nodded and waved. I felt Jacob's eyes on me as I followed Eric out of the theater.

Eric and I finished the final sips of our sodas and tossed the cups with the rest of our trash. He took my hand and we left the noisy media center. I breathed in the chilly spring air, just glad to be out of the theater.

"I thought I wanted to see a movie," I said. "But I really just wanted to talk to you!"

"Me too. I'm glad you wanted to leave."

We walked down the well-lit sidewalk and stopped

in front of the Sweet Shoppe—the campus's delicious café/bakery. I loved the sign with typewriter font that hung over the doorway.

"I have to run in here to get something," Eric said. "It's a surprise."

"A surprise?" I asked.

"Yeah. There's somewhere I want to take you after this."

I looked at his face—his eyes were sparkling even in the weak streetlamp light.

"I love surprises."

Eric squeezed my hand and released it. "Be right back."

He hurried into the Sweet Shoppe and I watched through the window, staring into the cozy shop. At a table near the back Julia and Alison sat together. They had a notebook in front of them and were scribbling things onto the paper, then whispering. When a sixth grader walked by, Julia moved her arm over the paper. I looked away from Julia and Alison when Eric exited the Sweet Shoppe carrying two big bags.

"Can I carry one?" I offered.

"I've got it," he said. "Interested in knowing where we're going?"

"Um, let me think." I paused, pretending to consider it. "Yes! Tell me!"

Eric laughed. I followed him down the sidewalk and away from the Sweet Shoppe.

"I thought we could have a picnic where we met."

"The stable," I said. "*Eric*. That's a great idea."

He smiled. "I had a feeling you'd like it."

We walked in comfortable silence to the stable. The lights had been dimmed and no one else was here.

"Are we allowed to be here?" I asked.

"I asked Mr. Conner yesterday," Eric said. "He's around here somewhere. He'll probably jump out from behind a hay bale if I try to kiss you." Eric whispered the last sentence.

I laughed. "He totally would."

"Let's go up to the hayloft," Eric said.

I followed him down the aisle. I went up the wooden ladder and reached the platform and . . . gasped at what I saw.

A tiny round table had been set up in the loft. The floor had been swept clean of hay. A battery-powered lantern added light to the space and a giant purple orchid blossomed in a vase on the table.

"How did you . . . ?" I couldn't finish my sentence.

"Mike and Doug," Eric said. "I told them I wanted to bring you here and they offered to bring the table and chairs up."

"Wow," I whispered. "That was so nice."

Eric put the Sweet Shoppe bags on the table and took my hand, leading me to the table. He pulled out my chair for me and I took my seat. The table was so tiny that our knees touched underneath.

Eric opened one white bag and took out two milkshakes—one chocolate and one chocolate-vanilla swirl. "I don't have to ask what one you want," he said, sliding the chocolate shake toward me.

"You know me too well." I accepted the chocolate shake and took a sip. Mmmm.

Eric opened the second bag and took out a wrapped foam plate. "New brownie recipe," he said. "I saw them put up the sign yesterday and knew you'd want to try it."

I stared hungrily at the brownies. "It's sad. I've eaten my weight in candy, but I'm dying for that brownie!"

Eric gave me a plate, fork, and napkin. "Here's the 'new' part," he said, reaching into the bag. He pulled out a little plastic container and opened it.

"Oh. My. God. Hot fudge," I said.

"Yep. To pour on the brownies."

I put a brownie on my plate and Eric did the same with his. "Go ahead," I said, motioning to him to use the fudge first. He drizzled it on his brownie and passed it to me. I poured way more onto mine, causing Eric to laugh.

We started eating and I closed my eyes. "Yum," I said. "This is the best. I love it."

I looked across the table at Eric—he was gazing at me.

"What?" I asked.

He scooted his chair around so he was beside me. We locked eyes—his face inches from mine. "You have a little chocolate on your face," he said.

I put a hand on my face. "Where?"

Eric reached up and touched the corner of my mouth with his thumb. "Here."

I think I stopped breathing. Eric put his hand on my cheek and my face warmed under his touch. My eyes fluttered shut and Eric's lips met mine. It was longer than we'd ever kissed and all I could taste was chocolate.

9

SHE'S LATE, SHE'S LATE! FOR A VIP DATE!

WHEN I SLID INTO MY SEAT AT BIO CLASS ON a sunny Monday morning, Julia and Alison didn't waste a second before they turned around to talk to me.

"Don't get used to us not being on the team," Julia snapped, tucking a lock of hair behind her ear. "This is just temporary."

"Julia, you cheated," I said. "And you got caught. Don't take it out on me." I was starting to feel a little annoyed by the whole thing.

A flush crept over Alison's face. "We didn't cheat," she whispered. "I swear."

"Stop trying to explain, Alison," Julia said, glaring at me. "Sasha loves this. It's less competition for the YENT."

I started to protest, but Jasmine walked into the room and took her seat next to me. She looked at me and simply rolled her eyes. I ignored her and stared ahead at the whiteboard. Finally, Ms. Peterson, our teacher, came into the room and stood in front of the class.

"Good morning, everyone," she said. "It's time for a Monday morning pop quiz."

We all groaned. I scribbled my name on my paper, thinking back to everything I'd read about the solar system over the weekend.

"Number one: name the lunar phases," Ms. Peterson said.

Got it. I wrote them down and looked up at Ms. Peterson when I finished.

"Number two: which planet is the smallest?" Ms. Peterson asked. She wrote tonight's homework on the whiteboard while she waited for us to answer.

I wrote down *Mercury*.

She asked a few more questions before telling us to put down our pens. "Please trade papers with the person sitting next to you," she said. "And you'll grade that person's quiz."

With a tiny sigh, I passed my paper to Jasmine. Ms. Peterson went through the correct answers and I handed

Jas back her paper with a minus one at the top. She gave me mine—also with one wrong. Last fall I'd probably have only gotten one right. I was glad I'd upped my studying more than usual—I refused to miss the YENT because of bad grades.

When I got to the stable for my afternoon lesson, I grabbed Charm's tack and grooming box before heading to his stall.

"Hi, gorgeous," I said to him, leading him into the wide aisle. Charm rubbed his forehead against my shoulder. "You're doing that because you're itchy, not because you love me, huh?" I teased.

I started grooming him and kept an eye on Jack's stall. Callie was usually here by now. We always groomed the horses together. I took out my phone.

Where r u? I texted her.

I'd finished grooming and tacking up Charm before my phone buzzed back.

Late! B there soon.

I wanted to wait for Callie, but Mr. Conner *hated* it when we weren't in class on time.

"We'd better go, boy," I told Charm.

We walked down the aisle and I mounted when I got

into the arena. Inside, Heather was circling Aristocrat at a trot. I moved Charm to the opposite end of the arena and walked him along the wall. It was weird to be in here with just Heather. I watched the door, hoping that Callie would manage to slip in before Mr. Conner got here. But when Mr. Conner strode through the doorway, Callie was still missing.

Mr. Conner didn't even pause. "Heather and Sasha, please do a sitting trot," he said. Heather and I urged our horses forward. I tried to keep my mind on the lesson, but I couldn't stop thinking about why Callie wasn't here. It had to be something major to keep her from practice.

"Sasha, lower your hands," Mr. Conner called. "And pay attention—you're pulling on Charm's mouth."

"Sorry," I whispered to Charm. I lowered my hands and held them still above the saddle.

"Shoulders back, Heather," Mr. Conner said.

He put his hands on his hips as he watched us circle around him. I looked up from between Charm's ears when I saw Callie trot Jack into the arena.

"I'm so sorry I'm late," she said to Mr. Conner, stopping Jack in front of him.

Callie was a mess. Half of her hair had escaped her ponytail and she had dry mud caked on her boots. I peered at Jack. She hadn't groomed him. Or, if she had, she'd missed the tangle in his mane and the bits of hay stuck in his tail.

"Callie, please leave," Mr. Conner said. "You know that I do not tolerate lateness and it appears that you didn't groom Jack prior to the lesson."

Callie lowered her head. "Sorry," she whispered.

"Please be on time for your next lesson and have Jack groomed properly."

Callie nodded. She dismounted and turned Jack away from us. She led him out of the arena. I wanted to go after Callie—I knew she must have felt awful. But I couldn't look for her until after the lesson.

Charm, confused by my lack of signals, weaved toward the wall—almost bumping Aristocrat.

"Pay attention, hello!" Heather hissed. Her blue eyes narrowed at me.

I nodded, letting Charm drop behind Aristocrat. Heather was right. I had to focus. Every practice between now and the YENT was crucial. I had to make each one count.

Mr. Conner worked with Heather and me for another forty minutes before dismissing us. I dismounted and hurried to get out of the arena.

Heather trotted Aristocrat in front of Charm and blocked the exit. "I'm *not* letting you mess this up," she snapped. "Callie was late and you're distracted. We all have to be focused and on our game or Jasmine King is going to think she has a chance at becoming the best Canterwood rider."

"Sorry," I said. "You're right."

With one last glare, Heather moved Aristocrat out of the way. The dark chestnut swished his tail in Charm's face as he walked forward. Heather guided him back to the wall and started doing a working trot.

"Aren't you leaving?" I asked.

Heather shook her head. "I'm practicing, Silver. Leave already."

She had to be as tired as I was after that grueling lesson. But she wasn't going to stop.

I unsnapped my helmet and led Charm out of the arena. Callie had Jack crosstied by the hot walker—his coat gleaming. She had also taken time to redo her ponytail.

"What happened?" I asked. "You're never late."

Callie put Jack's body brush into his red tack box. "I went to Jacob's track practice after class. I just totally forgot what time it was."

"Just don't do it again or Mr. Conner will be making

you run laps around the arena," I said, only half joking.

Callie unclipped Jack's crossties. "No kidding."

I loosened Charm's girth, preparing to cool him down. "If you see Heather, watch out. She gave me the 'if you lose focus and Jas makes the team and we don't, I'll kill you' speech."

"Not happening," Callie said. "We're totally focused."

10

WHO'S THE REAL
RIDER?

"WHY ISN'T TODAY FRIDAY?" I ASKED.

"Seriously," Callie said, linking her arm through mine. "How can it only be Wednesday?"

We walked down the hallway of the English building on our way to class. Sunlight streamed through the arched windows, catching the stained glass panes at the top. Spots of blue, red, and yellow hit the eggshell-white walls and swirled marble floor.

Laughter rang through the hallway and Callie stopped, yanking on my arm.

"Ow! What's—" I closed my mouth when I saw why she'd stopped.

Violet, Brianna, Georgia, and Jasmine stood in the middle of the hallway, huddled together and laughing.

"They're everywhere," Callie whispered. "I'm sick of running into them every five minutes."

"At least Jasmine doesn't live in *your* dorm," I said.

Callie looked behind us. "Let's go that way and circle back. They'll probably be gone by then."

We turned and walked away from them. "Everything okay?" I asked. "You're kind of jumpy today."

We peered down the hallway, checking to make sure the Belles and Jasmine had disappeared. The hallway was empty, so we stopped in front of our English classroom.

"Things with Jacob are a little . . . weird," Callie said. "He's been kind of distant. I know he's probably just stressed about school, but . . ."

"Probably," I said. "I mean, finals are coming up and I saw the track schedule in the gym. I bet he's going to be really busy."

Callie nodded. "Exactly. But Sash, I hope it's okay to say this . . . Jacob is so amazing. I had no idea I could fall for a guy like this."

"Of *course* you can say it. I feel the same way about Eric," I said. "And I was such a dork. I missed how great Eric was for so long." I loved that Callie and I could have a conversation about Eric and Jacob minus any old weirdness.

Callie giggled. "At least we finally figured it out."

I shifted my messenger bag strap. "I'm glad you're happy."

"I am. I just want to make sure—"

Our classroom door opened. Mr. Davidson popped his head into the hallway and saw us standing together. "C'mon, girls," he said, waving us into the classroom. "Class is about to start."

He held open the door for us and Callie and I went into the classroom. I'd try to assure Callie after class that things were fine with Jacob. He *was* probably stressed— like we all were.

"Ouch," I grumbled to Eric. He rode Luna over to me, frowning. I'd just finished a supergrueling lesson, but had agreed to practice more with Eric. I'd been waiting for him in the stable yard.

"Tough lesson?" Eric asked.

"My legs are going to fall off." I took my feet out of the stirrups and dangled them against Charm's sides.

Eric edged Luna closer. The flea-bitten gray mare had a definite crush on Charm. She touched her muzzle to his and I smiled at them.

"We can skip our practice if you want," Eric said. "No big deal if you're too tired."

"I *am* tired, but I need the practice. And so does Charm. The YENT keeps getting closer and I'll have less time once finals start."

We let the horses walk. "And my test for the advanced team is four days away," Eric said.

"Don't even worry about that." I turned to face him. "You're going to make it. C'mon. Let's take turns playing Mr. Conner. I'll coach you first."

Eric grinned. "Cool."

"Let's go to the practice cross-country course."

We rode the horses across the grassy yard and I unbuttoned my jacket. It was warmer than usual today and Charm was loving it. He almost pranced through the grass, eager to start jumping.

I eyed the short course Mr. Conner had designed for us so we could practice without being too far away from the stable.

"I think you should take the gate, the two brush jumps, the coffin and the stone wall. Then trot down the hill and circle back to me."

Eric nodded. "Works for me." He settled into Luna's saddle before letting her into a trot. They started up the gentle hill and I watched them, shading my eyes with my hand. Eric bounced a little as Luna bounded up the last few strides of the hill. She reached level ground and her canter quickened. Eric urged her toward the gate and she soared over it. He slowed her a notch and she swished her tail, annoyed, but listened to him. He got her over the first brush jump and then pointed her at the second.

I half stood in the saddle, keeping my eyes on his hands, legs, and seat. His legs slid back and his knees weren't tight enough against the saddle.

Eric cantered Luna to the second line of brush, but Luna lost focus and started to weave. She slowed and Eric didn't react in time to get her momentum up. Luna jumped, but her back hooves dragged over the top of the brush.

"Tighten your knees!" I called.

Eric must have heard me because his legs went back into the correct position and he urged Luna into a faster canter. She didn't even blink at the coffin and it gave her confidence to leap the stone wall.

"Great finish!" I cheered as Eric rode over to me.

"She almost refused the brush jump," Eric said, shaking his head. "Advice?"

"Not enough pressure," I said. "Your signals were lax, too, and you wobbled in the saddle. Luna used that as an excuse and she looked like she thought about ducking out."

"I lost focus for a second," Eric admitted. "That's dangerous on a cross-country course."

I circled Charm, readying him to go. "It is, but at least you're aware of it. You'll stay more focused next time."

Eric nodded, taking a breath. "Okay, cross-country superstar, it's your turn."

I sank my weight into the saddle and trotted Charm forward. I was glad there wasn't a creek around this part of campus. I didn't want to mess up in front of Eric. But I still had to fix Charm's water phobia.

"I'll take you out to the water with Callie and Jack," I said to Charm as we reached the top of the hill. "We'll fix it."

Charm didn't need any urging to canter. He leaped forward, his strides eating the grass. He powered over the old gate. That felt *so* good! I guided him over both brush jumps and Charm wasn't a bit winded as he cantered around a long turn and approached the coffin. The coffin—a ditch with rails on both sides—required a slower canter. Sometimes, Mr. Conner filled the ditch with water, but it was empty today. I collected Charm, preparing him for the wide spread.

He slowed and I squeezed my knees against the saddle. Charm surged forward and stretched as he cleared the rails and ditch. He landed with his hooves inches from the jump.

"Nice," I whispered to him. "One more!"

We reached the stone wall in seconds and wind whooshed in my ears as Charm lifted into the air. He'd taken off a half second too late and had to tuck his forelegs tighter under his body to avoid touching the wall with his hooves.

"Not bad, boy," I said, patting his neck and slowing him to a trot.

"You guys make it look easy," Eric said.

I shook my head. "We took off too late before the wall."

"Forget about it," Eric said. "It's show jumping time."

I laughed when I saw the gleam in his eye. "You love playing Mr. Conner, don't you?" I asked.

After our ride I led a cooled Charm down the aisle and passed Julia and Alison, who were grooming Trix and Sunstruck. They both saw me and glared before looking away. It had to be insanely difficult to be around horses but not be able to ride. I couldn't even think about the possibility of not riding Charm till next January.

"Is Mr. Conner softening at all about letting you ride?" I asked, turning back to them.

"Yeah, right," Julia huffed. "Alison and I are in his office, like, every other day telling him we're innocent. But he doesn't believe us."

"At least you get to see your horses. Imagine if you'd been banned from the stable."

Julia raised her eyebrows. "That makes me feel *so* much better. Thanks a ton."

Alison put down Sunstruck's currycomb and folded her arms. "Maybe it would have been easier. Then we wouldn't have to watch everyone else ride."

"Sorry," I said, walking Charm forward. "I wasn't trying to make you feel worse."

I released Charm into his stall and he went straight to his hay net. "Bye, boy."

I walked toward the Sweet Shoppe for my midweek cookie break and texted Paige.

Almost @ SS. Want anything?

She texted back. *No thanx. Just made brownies.*

Hmmm . . . Paige's brownies were better than the Sweet Shoppe's. But I felt like iced coffee after that ride. I walked toward the shop, deleting old texts as I walked. I looked up and stopped midstep.

Jasmine and Heather stood in front of the shop, facing one another. Both girls had their arms crossed and eyes locked on each other. Jasmine was dressed for riding in white breeches, black boots and a fly-away sweater coat. Heather looked ready for a date in a double-breasted green pea coat, black skirt, and peep toe shoes.

I decided just to keep walking.

"Sasha," Jasmine called. "Don't run away so fast."

I turned to look at her. "I'm *not* running anywhere. I'm going inside."

Jasmine shook her head. "But you should hear this. Your teammate Heather is trying to convince me of some-thing superfunny."

My eyes flickered from Heather to Jasmine. "What?" I asked.

"I'm not convincing her of anything," Heather said, her face a deep shade of pink. "I'm *assuring* her that we—the real Canterwood riders—will make the YENT. Jasmine won't. Right?"

I just stood there, annoyed to be in the middle of their fight. "We don't know who's going to make it," I said. "But I guess the scouts will pick the best riders for the team. We all have a shot."

Jasmine, tilting her head to look at me sideways, laughed.

"You're delusional," she said. "Perfect example—just look at us. Who's in riding clothes?"

I just stared at her, not answering.

"*I* am," Jasmine continued. "Because I'm actually on my way back to practice more. Heather's not. Obvi. And, if I had to guess, I'd say you're here to stuff your face with cookies."

"I just finished practicing," I said. "Not that I have to explain myself to you."

Jasmine started toward the stable. "Oh, you don't have to," she said. "I'm just fine with you not making the YENT."

Heather took a deep breath and shook her head once Jasmine was gone. "I'm going to totally—"

"Don't," I said. "She's not even worth it. We're doing everything we can for the YENT. You know it. She's just trying to throw us off our game."

Heather threw up a hand. "She doesn't even need to try. Our team is a disaster as it is."

"What are you talking about?"

"Really? Let's see . . . ," Heather put a finger to her chin. "Callie was late and she got kicked out for looking like a slob, Julia and Alison are so furious, they can barely function . . . and aren't allowed to ride anyway.

And now *I'm* getting distracted because of *her*. I'm done. I'm going to change and go ride."

Heather stomped away from me before I could say anything else. I stood there, staring longingly at the Sweet Shoppe. But I turned away and walked toward Winchester. Paige's brownies were better anyway and I needed to do my homework.

Suddenly, Heather had me feeling insecure about everything I'd been doing—or not doing.

11

PRESSURE COOKER

MR. CONNER CAME INTO THE OUTDOOR ARENA for our afternoon lesson and nodded when he saw we were all there on time. Ever since she'd been late, Callie had been sure to be the first one in the arena.

Mr. Conner put us through a long dressage lesson and my arms ached after repeat attempts to collect Charm's trot and canter.

"Great job, everyone," Mr. Conner said. "Please dismount and cool your horses. See you next class."

I dismounted and walked Charm over to Jack. "Good ride," I said to Callie. "Ready to go again?" I made a pretend-serious face.

"Totally." She mock-rolled her eyes. "You first."

We walked side by side as we cooled the horses.

"Paige is spending the night at Geena's," I said.

"Her friend from cooking class?"

I nodded. "They're watching *Teen Cuisine* together. Do you want to sleep over?"

Callie smiled. "Only if TV, movies, and tons of junk food are involved."

"Of course," I said, feeling Charm's neck to see if he was cool. "Those are, like, essentials."

"Cool. I'll come over after your film class."

We started the last turn around the arena to cool out the horses. As we walked I couldn't help thinking how weeks ago, a sleepover with Callie had seemed as if it would never happen again. But our friendship kept getting better and I knew we'd get back to being super BFFs before we left for summer vacay.

On my way out of the stable I passed the indoor arena and stopped when I saw a horse and rider flash by the window. Heather moved Aristocrat along the wall, sitting quietly to his canter. She was *still* practicing?

I walked into the arena and when Heather turned Aristocrat back, she saw me. She focused her gaze forward again, ignoring me and slowing Aristocrat to a trot. She trotted him past me and through the arena's center. She sat for a beat as Aristocrat crossed through the diagonal and she got back on the right lead. She worked for ten minutes before she asked him for a walk. Aristocrat took sharp breaths and sweat had darkened his chest.

"He looks happy to quit," I called out.

Heather stopped him in front of me and pushed her helmet back. "We're not done."

"We just had a lesson and you've been in here for at least an hour by yourself," I said. "Aristocrat's tired."

Heather rubbed his neck. "I'm giving him a break, Silver. Chill."

I looked closer at Heather. She had a smudge on her chin and faint circles under her eyes. Her cheeks looked a little hollowed.

"Plus, you probably have something else you want to do tonight," I said. "It's Friday, right?"

Heather glared at me. "Go bother someone else, okay? I need to finish up here."

I walked out of the arena, shaking my head. When I turned the corner, I almost ran right into Alison. She looked out of place in the stable with her skinny jeans, paddock boots, and sparkly purple T-shirt.

"Have you seen Heather?" she asked.

"Indoor arena," I said. "Still practicing."

"Oh." Alison frowned. "Okay."

She started to walk away, but I called after her. "Is something wrong with Heather?"

Alison turned back to me. She stuck her hands in her pockets. "Like what?"

"She just seems superstressed. And she has to be tired, but she's still riding." I shrugged. "Just asking."

Alison looked as if she was going to blow me off. But then she stepped closer to me. "She's just stressed, like you said. There's a lot of pressure."

"Her dad?" I guessed.

Alison's eyes widened slightly. "Yeah. It's always her dad. But whatever, I don't know why I'm telling *you* this. Not like you care."

"Heather's my teammate," I said, brushing a Charm hair off my jacket sleeve. "Believe it or not, I want her to do well. And I'm not going to tell anyone that we talked—I swear."

Alison looked at her boots, then back at me. "I can't believe I'm about to continue this conversation, but I do feel bad for Heather. Her dad told her if she didn't make the YENT, he was going to sell Aristocrat and make her transfer to another boarding school."

"He's threatening her with *that* again?" Mr. Fox had

made the same threats last fall if Heather didn't make the advanced team.

"Yeah. And she's worried. I mean, last time she knew she'd likely make the advanced team. But making the YENT is so much harder."

I leaned against the wall, trying to think of a way to help. "Anything we can do?"

Alison gave me a half smile. "I haven't thought of anything yet. Maybe I'll go offer to coach her tomorrow if she agrees to stop for today."

I nodded. "Good idea."

As I walked to Winchester, I tried to imagine my parents taking Charm away from me. I couldn't even go there. Heather and I had our problems, but I didn't want to see her lose Aristocrat.

12

THAT RINGTONE

FILM CLASS WAS STARTING IN TWO MINUTES
and Jacob still hadn't shown. I shifted in my cushy red
seat and tapped my fingers on the armrest.

Mr. Ramirez stood in front of the class and smiled at
us. He always started film class with a quote and it was
like a class competition to see who could get it right first.
"'I have a brilliant beyond brilliant idea!'"

I knew it! "*The Parent Trap!*" I called out.

Mr. Ramirez nodded. "Nice, Sasha."

Where was Jacob? He never skipped class. And Callie
hadn't said a word about him being sick or anything.

"Today, we'll be talking about original films versus
remakes," Mr. Ramirez said. "We'll watch the 1961 version of *The Parent Trap* and then you'll watch the remake

on your own over the weekend. I'll assign homework for the films and you'll complete it after you've watched both movies."

While he started to set up the movie, I texted Jacob. I couldn't help it—I was worried.

U ok? I sent the text and applied a layer of maple syrup–flavored gloss.

But fifteen minutes later, he still hadn't texted back. I thought about texting Callie, but didn't want her to think it was weird that I was checking up on her boyfriend. I sat through the rest of the movie, barely able to concentrate. When Mr. Ramirez finally dismissed the class, I hurried back to Winchester.

You'd know if something was going on, I told myself. *Callie would have told you.* I was still thinking about it when Callie arrived at my room.

"Hey!" she said. "I brought an insane amount of candy. We'll totally crash after we eat all of it."

"That's *exactly* what I wanted to hear," I said. I took the bag she handed me and peered inside as she opened her backpack. "Niiice." I looked at the bags of M&M's (peanut and plain), candy bars, and a giant bag of jelly beans.

"There was more, but I gave Jacob a giant Hershey's bar before I came over."

I unwrapped a Twix. "I was wondering why he wasn't in film class. So he was skipping to hang out with you?" I shook my head in pretend disapproval.

Callie reached into the bag, pulling out an Almond Joy.

"He wasn't skipping—he had an excuse," she said. "He hurt his knee in gym and was supposed to ice it for the rest of the night."

"Ouch." I put down my candy bar. "Sorry."

Callie stuck out her bottom lip. "I feel so bad for him. But he'll be okay."

I flicked on the TV. "He totally will be. But be careful—he might start getting 'injured' more often just so you bring him candy."

Callie laughed. She flopped onto her stomach on Paige's bed and faced the TV. "What's on the schedule for tonight?"

I tossed her the list of possibilities I'd made during math class. "Pick something."

Callie scanned the list, nodding at some of the choices. I fluffed my pillows and eased back onto them, stretching out on my bed. I'd just gotten comfortable when my phone rang. I almost fell off my bed when I heard *the* ringtone.

I sat up, glancing at the phone and then at Callie.

"You can get it," she said. "It's gonna take me another minute to pick something."

I snatched up my phone. "Hello?" I asked, pretending as if my caller ID was broken.

"Uh, hey. It's Jacob."

"Hi," I said. Callie looked over at me, then back at the list.

"Sorry to call if you're busy or something, but I really need to talk to you."

"Why?" For a second, I forgot Callie was even here. Jacob sounded superstrange.

"Look, I'm sorry about how weird things have been. There's just . . . something I need to tell you. I—"

Whoa! This was not going to be a good conversation to have right in front of Callie.

"Callie's here!" I half shouted. "Callie's here and we have to watch our movie."

Callie glanced up from the list, looking at me with a why-are-you-yelling face. I turned away from her, letting my hair fall into my face.

"Oh." Jacob paused and took a breath. "Never mind. It was nothing. Can you e-mail me the homework from film?"

"Yep," I squeaked. "I'll e-mail it to you."

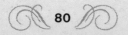

"Thanks. Bye." Jacob hung up and I shut off my phone before putting it beside my bed.

"That was Jacob," I said. I wasn't going to lie to Callie about who was on the phone. "He wanted the homework for film."

Callie nodded, her eyes lingering on my phone for a second before she pulled her hair into a high ponytail. "Okay."

I waited for her to be upset that Jacob had called me, but she seemed cool. "So, what did you pick?"

"The new Bryce Oliver movie. For sure."

"Let's get into PJs, grab sodas and popcorn, and start the movie."

We got into our pajamas and fuzzy socks. For the first time in months, it felt like Callie and I were BFFs pre–The Jacob-and-Eric Mess.

You totally overreacted about Jacob's phone call, I told myself. Whatever he'd wanted to tell me—it didn't matter. There was nothing he had to say that was important right now. Callie and I were having fun together and it was about time.

A couple of hours later the movie was over and my eyes kept fluttering shut.

"Ugh, I feel like such a grandma," I said. "It's not even midnight and I'm exhausted."

"Me too." Callie yawned. "I'm ready to crash."

I turned off the TV and we got settled into our beds. "What are you doing tomorrow?"

"I'm not hanging out with Jacob till the afternoon," Callie said. "So I'm on my own. You?"

"Eric's got a bio lab session with his partner in the morning, then he'll be practicing for the advanced team."

"Want to do something together?" Callie asked.

We looked at each other and I *knew* we were thinking the same thing.

"Trail ride!" we said at the same time.

"No practicing," I said.

"And no worrying about the YENT," Callie finished.

I turned off the light and fell against my pillow with a happy sigh. In seconds, my eyes closed and I drifted off to sleep, glad to have Callie as my friend again. One hundred percent.

13

SHOWDOWN

BY EIGHT THE NEXT MORNING, CALLIE AND
I were at the stable. We hurried through tacking up the
horses, chatting and laughing the whole time. We led
them outside and I squinted from the bright sunshine.

"I'm still disgustingly full of junk food," Callie said, as
we walked beside Charm and Jack. We stopped the horses
and mounted.

"Me too. I think we should stick to a walk for a while."

We let the horses amble toward the woods. I gave
Charm a loose rein and relaxed in the saddle.

"Trail riding was only the best idea ever," Callie said.
"I was getting bored with practicing."

I nodded. "Imagine how Charm and Jack feel. They . . ."
I let my sentence trail off when the small outdoor arena

came into view. Heather and Jasmine were at opposite ends of the arena, cantering Aristocrat and Phoenix.

Callie and I halted the horses, stopping before Jas or Heather noticed us. Heather, sneaking a glance at Jasmine, turned Aristocrat sharply toward the arena's center. Jasmine guided Phoenix in the same direction. Both girls cantered the horses down the center of the arena, only feet apart from being on the same track. They swept past each other and turned when they reached the ends of the arena. Phoenix kicked up a clump of dirt as Jasmine pulled him to a halt.

The girls stared at each other before Jasmine urged Phoenix into a trot. She sat to his smooth gait and moved him around the outer edge of the arena, heading for Heather. Heather let Aristocrat trot and sat, too, mirroring Jasmine's actions. Jasmine eyed Heather and collected Phoenix's trot. Heather did the same. It was turning into an all-out arena battle.

"I know we should go before they catch us," Callie whispered. "But I can't stop watching."

"Me either."

Heather halted Aristocrat and backed him in a perfect straight line. Jasmine stopped Phoenix, asking him to back up, and took him three steps farther back than Heather had done with Aristocrat.

Heather trotted Aristocrat up to Phoenix and halted him when she was side-by-side with Jasmine.

"Uh-oh," I said. Charm pointed his ears toward the arena and raised his head. He didn't want to miss a word, either.

"Not good," Callie said.

"Let's go!" I said. "Just trot them past the arena and talk and pretend we didn't see a thing."

Callie started to nod, then stopped. "Forget that."

I glanced back at the arena. Heather's eyes were on us.

"Go!" I whispered.

Callie and I trotted the horses and stared at the woods, not wanting to look at Heather or Jasmine.

"Wait a sec," Heather called out to us. "You two were obviously waiting for a show. You should stay."

"It's okay," I said quickly. "We're going on a trail ride."

Heather twisted in the saddle to stare us down. "Well then, you need to wait. I want you both to hear exactly what I'm going to say to Jas."

Now I was too curious to ride away. Callie and I slowed the horses and rode them up to the fence.

Heather turned Aristocrat away from us and stopped him next to Phoenix. Jasmine, sitting tall in the saddle, readjusted her grip on Phoenix's reins. Callie and I traded glances.

"I have a few things I wanted to say," Heather said, her voice sharp. "And *you* need to listen."

That was the old Heather I loved to hate. Jasmine's shoulders slumped a little and she seemed to lose a bit of her cockiness from minutes earlier.

"Heather," Jasmine moaned. "Stop being such a drama queen and just talk."

Heather's eyes zeroed in on Jasmine's face. "Unfortunately for you, the drama's just getting started. We all know that you'll make the advanced team tomorrow. Given."

Jasmine rolled her eyes. "Obvi."

"But we're not going to hand you a spot on the YENT. Callie, Sasha, and I are going to make sure that we ride so well, the scouts won't even *consider* you."

"You really think you're better than *I* am?" Jas asked.

Heather smiled. "I don't think. I *know*." She dug her left heel into Aristocrat's side, spinning him away from Phoenix. Within three strides, he broke into a canter and they made their way down the center of the arena and out the exit.

"I guess that's our cue," I said to Callie.

Jasmine glared at us as we turned the horses away from the arena and trotted them toward the woods. We didn't say a word until we were yards down the trail and the trees closed in behind us.

We pulled the horses to a walk. "*That* was intense," I said.

"No kidding," Callie said. She rubbed Jack's neck with one hand. "But in a weird way, I'm kind of glad to see her like that."

I nodded. "The *old* Heather."

We guided the horses down the dirt trail and I pushed up the sleeves of my royal blue jacket. "Maybe she'll rattle Jasmine enough that she messes up the YENT tryouts. We both know Heather's right about Jas making the advanced team."

"For sure. And I have to admit . . . I feel sorry for Julia and Alison. It's awful that they had to give up their spots."

"And they already hated Jas. It has to be killing them that they can't ride, but she can."

Callie gave Jack more rein and let him stretch his neck. "*I'd* die. But I don't think Jack would miss the crazy workouts."

"Charm wouldn't either. He's just a laid-back guy." Charm snorted and I patted his shoulder.

Callie and I exited the woods and walked the horses along the grassy lane near the stone wall.

"But, worst-case scenario," Callie said. "We have to think about it."

"No, we don't. No. Don't even say it."

"We have to. It could happen," Callie said. "What if . . ."

"Ugh—I sooo don't even want to think about this!"

Callie looked at me. "What if Jasmine makes the team and none of us do?"

For a few seconds, the only sound I heard was Jack's and Charm's hooves striking the grass.

"If she's the only one who makes it," I said, "it's simple."

"It is?" Callie asked.

I nodded, looking nonchalant. "Yep. We transfer to Wellington."

Callie laughed and I shook my head. "You think I'm kidding?" I tried to look serious, but my smile gave me away.

"It's a deal," Callie said, holding out a pinky finger. "If Jas is the only one to make it, Wellington here we come."

I linked my pinky to Callie's, desperately hoping we'd never call Wellington our home.

We reached a wide part of the creek and I pulled Charm up.

"C'mon," Callie said. "You have to get him over his water fear before the YENT cross-country."

"I know, but he *really* hates it. I feel bad making him get in the water when he doesn't want to."

Callie walked Jack toward the creek. "Don't get soft on me, Sasha Silver. Let's go!"

"Okay. Let's walk them side by side."

I let Charm catch up with Jack and the horses bobbed their heads, relaxed and content, as they walked toward the creek. Strides before we reached the water, I tensed in the saddle, expecting Charm to balk. Jack, not even looking at the creek bed, stepped into the water. Charm leaned back and dug his heels into the soft dirt.

"Charm, c'mon." I tapped him with my heels and tried to push him forward with my seat.

Callie turned Jack around and walked him back across the creek to us. She steadied him beside Charm and leaned over, taking the left rein.

"I'll pony you across," she said. She clicked to Jack and she led Charm. Charm's ears flicked back and forth and he trembled as he stepped into the water with his right foreleg. Then he bounded ahead, taking huge strides to get out of the creek as fast as possible. He jerked the rein out of Callie's hand and I snatched it up.

"Easy," I said, gripping his mane so I didn't slip backward.

He trotted up the bank and shook his head, his chestnut mane flying. Callie and Jack followed us calmly.

"That was awful!" I said.

Callie shook her head. "It wasn't awful. He'll get over it—we'll help him. But . . ." She stopped.

"But what?" I adjusted the stirrup I'd almost lost when Charm had made his mad dash.

"I think Charm would have gone over the creek, but you tensed before he hit the water. I think he could feel your nerves."

"Oh." I nodded, thinking. "You're right. I did tense up. I knew he was scared and I should have made him feel confident."

Callie leaned forward, adjusting Jack's mane. "You'll get it. No worries."

But I couldn't stop worrying as we finished our ride. I *had* to help Charm get over his water phobia before the YENT trials. There was no way we'd make it if Charm refused to go through a creek.

14

TEAM ERIC

IT WAS BARELY SEVEN WHEN I GOT TO THE stable. I walked down the aisle, swallowing back a yawn and looking for Eric.

A few stalls down, Mr. Conner stood in the aisle and looked at his clipboard. "Sasha," he said when he saw me. "Come into my office for a second?"

"Okay." I followed him, trying to think if I'd done something wrong. Jasmine was already sitting in front of his desk. She smirked at me as I took my seat. She'd done something. Something bad. I just knew it.

Mr. Conner sat behind his big wooden desk and leaned back in his chair for a second, looking at both of us. My heart thumped uncomfortably. If Jasmine got me in trouble for something I didn't do . . .

"Sasha," Mr. Conner said. "I asked to speak with you because I have news about the YENT. News I'm sure you'll be excited to hear."

I nodded. Maybe this *wasn't* something bad . . .

"I've already told Jasmine and she said that you were both best friends now and that you'd want her here when I told you."

I tried to speak, to say that Jasmine and I were not even *close* to best friends, but nothing came out.

"Sasha, you'll be glad to know that your best friend is the most wonderful rider," Mr. Conner said. "When Jasmine arrived at Canterwood, I felt as though I'd finally gotten the perfect equestrian. Jasmine is the best rider Canterwood has ever had. And unfortunately, she makes you look even less experienced than you already are."

I almost fell off my chair. Tears blurred my vision and my face felt hot. How could he be saying these things to me?!

Mr. Conner locked eyes with me, his face showing no trace of sympathy. "I want to spend more time working with Jasmine and the YENT scouts agreed that she needs extra attention. We're going to remove you from the advanced team, Sasha, and are placing you with the beginners."

"What?" I managed to gasp.

"Jasmine is the only rider at Canterwood who even has a chance at making the YENT, so I don't want to waste my time on a rider who can't."

I jumped up, knocked over my chair, and bolted for the door. I started sobbing and grasped the door handle, barely able to see through my tears. *This was not happening. It—*

"Sasha?" A hand gently shook my shoulder.

"What?" I opened my eyes and looked up at Paige. She was leaning over my bed, her worried eyes flickering over my face. The lamp was on in our room and it was still dark outside.

"You were having a nightmare. You started crying," Paige said. "It's okay. I'm right here."

"Oh, my God," I said, letting out a shuddering breath. "I thought it was real! Mr. Conner told me he was putting me on the beginner team and that Jasmine was the best rider at Canterwood."

Paige sat on the side of my bed. "That's so not true. And you're waaay too good for the beginner team. You know that."

I nodded as my heart rate returned to normal. I brushed my sweaty hair from my forehead and gave Paige a small smile. "I'm sorry I woke you. I'm okay now." I checked the clock—five forty-five. "I'm just going to stay up."

Paige got up from my bed and flipped on the overhead light. "I'm awake too. We can get to the caf before all of the good muffins are gone."

We showered, dressed, and went to breakfast. Paige, happy with the morning selection, grabbed two banana nut muffins and I took two chocolate chip muffins. We had plenty of time to eat before I had to get to the stable to help Eric with Luna.

We sat at our usual table and Paige sipped her orange/cranberry juice mix. "So, what's with the nightmares?" she asked.

I thought for a minute. "I'm just worried about finals . . . and the YENT," I confessed. "I want to make that team."

"First, you've totally got finals under control," Paige said, putting down her glass. "Think about where you were last semester compared to this one. You're studying as much as you can and that's all you can do. I know you'll do well."

I nibbled a chocolate chip off my muffin.

"And second, you're ready for the YENT. You'd make it if they tested you today. You're a great rider, Sash. You don't give yourself enough credit."

"Thanks, Paige. You're a good roomie."

"You can totally pay me back by watching the next

Teen Cuisine episode with me on Friday," Paige said.

"It's a date. And, seriously, how high are the ratings? Is every single person in America watching your show?"

Paige blushed. "My producer did say the ratings were good . . ."

"And?" I prodded.

"And twice as high as last season," Paige admitted, turning even pinker.

"Paige! That's awesome. But I'm not surprised."

We talked about *Teen Cuisine* for the rest of breakfast and the anxiety of the nightmare slowly ebbed away.

By the time I got to the stable, Eric was already there with Luna in crossties. I passed Phoenix's empty stall— Jasmine was testing now.

"Hey," I said, giving Eric a quick hug. "How're you feeling?"

He smiled, but it wasn't a real Eric smile. "Just a little nervous."

I grabbed a comb from Luna's tack box and started detangling her tail. "The nerves will turn into adrenaline when you're in the arena. I know you're going to do great."

We slipped into silence as we groomed. I knew Eric needed time to think and concentrate. While we groomed

Luna, I thought about *my* upcoming test and how it would determine my entire summer. I'd either go home for a couple of weeks before going to YENT camp, or I'd be home *all* summer. And what about Eric? I watched him, his face serious as he bridled Luna. What about *us*?

"Here," I said, taking Luna's reins. "I'll hold Luna while you get her saddled."

My worries about my own riding future disappeared as I held Luna. All of my concentration went to Eric.

He finished tightening the girth and ran down the stirrups. Holding his black helmet under one arm, he turned to me. "Any tips?"

I took his hand. "Just pretend it's any other lesson. You've worked *so* hard for this, Eric. You'll kill it!"

Eric stepped closer to me, squeezing my hand.

"Eric?" Mike said, walking down the aisle toward us. "You're up." He offered a fist to Eric for a nudge. "Good luck."

"Thanks."

Mike walked away and I led Luna toward the indoor arena while Eric put on his helmet. He got in the saddle and looked down at me.

"I'll be cheering you on from the skybox," I said.

"You better."

He rode into the arena as Jasmine exited. I started walking toward the skybox, hoping to get away before she could comment about something.

"Your boyfriend is gonna need lots of luck to make the team," she called after me.

I ignored her and walked up the stairs. When I opened the door, I found Andy, Ben, Troy, and Nicole waiting. They were all friends of mine and Eric's, and riders on the intermediate team.

Nicole patted the seat next to her, brushing blond hair off her heart-shaped face. "Sit," she said.

I sat beside her and we waved at Eric when he looked up at us. I knew he had to feel good about having friends cheering for him. The skybox had been empty for Jasmine. The Belles, her so-called "friends," hadn't even bothered to show up.

"He's definitely going to make it," Ben said. "I rode with him yesterday and he was great."

Eric warmed up Luna along the wall, taking her from a trot to a canter. He'd dressed up for the test in a black jacket, new breeches, and his show boots.

My phone buzzed. *Txt me aftr E's test. I knw he'll mke it!*

Callie. I texted back. *Will do!!*

The skybox door opened and I expected to see Jasmine.

But Rachel and her friends walked inside. Nicole shot me a what-are-*they*-doing-here glance. I shrugged. Then glossed.

"Hey, Sasha," Rachel said sweetly.

"Hey," I said, my voice faltering slightly. Rachel was really pretty—and were those highlights in her hair?

The girls grabbed the last few seats and peered down at Eric. They started whispering and giggling. *Whatever,* I said to myself. *Don't get jealous. Eric's with you.*

Mr. Conner walked into the arena and glanced up at the skybox, seeming surprised when he saw all of us. "Not a word from any of you," he said to us. "Understand?"

We nodded. Mr. Conner walked into the center of the arena and Eric slowed Luna to a walk.

"Let's get started, if you're ready," Mr. Conner said. "Follow my directions and you'll do fine. Good luck."

Eric nodded and urged Luna toward the wall. I scooted to the edge of my seat and crossed my fingers. Nicole, glancing at my hands, did the same.

"Sitting trot," Mr. Conner called. Eric sat to Luna's trot, not bouncing at all. His hands stayed low over Luna's neck, his heels were down and he was balanced over the saddle. *Perfect.*

"Posting trot," Mr. Conner said. He jotted something on his clipboard. Eric posted for two laps around the arena.

Luna, quiet under Eric, listened to every command.

I glanced over at Rachel and her friends. They were perched at the edges of their seats with their eyes stuck on Eric.

"Cross over the center and reverse direction," Mr. Conner called. Eric turned Luna toward the arena's center and sat for a beat when he crossed the halfway point of the arena and started to turn in the opposite direction. He made another lap going counterclockwise.

"Halt," Mr. Conner called.

Within strides, Eric pulled Luna to a smooth stop.

"He's got this," Nicole whispered to me. I nodded, never taking my eyes off Eric.

Mr. Conner put Eric through several more exercises before he raised his hand. "Walk, please," Mr. Conner called.

Eric slowed Luna and patted her shoulder. When Mr. Conner looked at his clipboard, I waved at Eric and gave him a thumbs up. He'd aced the flatwork part of the test.

"I'd like you to take Luna over those four jumps," Mr. Conner said, pointing to the opposite end of the arena. "You may start whenever you're ready."

I took a deep breath, but knew I didn't have to worry about Eric's jumping unless something crazy happened. He was the best jumper at school.

Eric walked Luna for a few more seconds before asking her to trot. He circled her twice and then urged her into a canter. Luna's red leg wraps flashed as she cantered, shaking her head playfully. Eric settled her and then set her up in front of the first red and white vertical.

I counted strides in my head and whispered, "Now!" at the same second Eric lifted in the saddle. Luna rose over the jump and landed cleanly on the other side. She cantered for eight strides before reaching the oxer. She gathered herself and jumped over the spread, her back hooves inches away from the rails.

"Two more," I whispered.

"He's got it," Ben said behind me.

Luna's speed increased a notch and Eric guided her to the combination. Eric only had two strides from the first jump of the combo to gather Luna and get her over the next jump. Combos were tricky.

Luna reached the first jump of the combination, with white rails that were about three and a half feet high, and leaped into the air. Eric was ready the second they were on the ground. He rose in the saddle at the right moment and Luna jumped the second half of the combination. I held my breath as she seemed to suspend in the air and I almost squeezed my eyes shut. But she landed on the other side, not even coming close to knocking the rail. The tense look on Eric's face vanished. He rubbed Luna's neck.

That had been a great ride! Eric couldn't have done any better.

Rachel and her friends clapped silently with their fingertips.

Mr. Conner wrote something on his clipboard. "Please dismount," he told Eric. Eric did and took off his helmet.

Mike came into the arena and took Luna from Eric. Mr. Conner motioned to Jasmine, who had appeared in the entrance. She walked over to stand beside Eric.

"Thank you for those excellent rides," Mr. Conner said. "You both impressed me with how much you've practiced since I scheduled your testing. I have no doubt that you're dedicated riders and I'm lucky to have you both in my stable."

I was so proud of Eric. He deserved to hear that— he'd been working nonstop since the testing had been scheduled.

"I don't need time to think about my decision," Mr. Conner continued. "You both have great potential and would make excellent additions to the advanced team. I'd like to welcome you with my congratulations."

I clapped my hand over my mouth to stop from shouting. Mr. Conner turned, looking up at the skybox. "You can cheer now," he said, shaking his head.

Eric laughed and smiled up at us.

Ben, Nicole, and I started clapping and cheering.

"Congratulations," Eric said, turning to Jasmine.

She stared at him, then seemed to remember that Mr. Conner was standing feet away. "You too," she said sweetly.

"Jasmine," Mr. Conner said. "I'm pleased that I was able to advance you this time. Keep up the work you're doing on becoming a softer rider."

Jasmine nodded and tucked a lock of wavy hair behind her ear. "I will, Mr. Conner."

"Good," Mr. Conner said. "I'll see both of you at seven tomorrow morning for practice. If you're interested in celebrating, there will be a cake at the Sweet Shoppe at two." He turned to the skybox and tilted his head toward us. "The cheering section is also invited."

We started laughing. "As if we'd miss cake," Ben called down to Mr. Conner.

Mr. Conner laughed and shook Eric's hand, then Jasmine's. "Congratulations."

Mr. Conner started toward the exit. He wasn't even three steps away from Eric and Jasmine when I was out of my seat and hurrying toward the arena. I ran across the dirt floor and grabbed Eric in a hug.

"Omigod!" I said. "Who was right?"

Eric stepped back, putting his hands on my waist. His warm brown eyes had their special Eric sparkle. "Hmm. I don't know . . . you, maybe?"

"Um, yeah," I teased. "I was totally right. I *knew* you'd make it!"

"Ewww," Jasmine said, shaking her head. I'd been so excited that I'd forgotten she was still there.

I pointed to the exit. "The door's that way," I said.

Jasmine crossed her arms. "Please. You are the ones who can take your disgusting 'Omigod!-You're-so-amazing,-Sasha!-No,-Eric,-you-are!' display elsewhere."

"Fine," I said lightly. I slipped my fingers through Eric's. "We will."

And without another word to Jasmine, my advanced team boyfriend and I left the arena hand in hand.

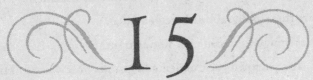

15

HOPE WE'RE
NOT TEAMMATES
FOR LONG

FOR THE FIRST PART OF THE AFTERNOON, Paige and I studied in the Winchester common room. I'd claimed the recliner and a pillow for my lap. Paige sat cross-legged in the window seat. She was writing an essay for English, I was doing math homework, and we'd already quizzed each other for our science classes.

"I've got to leave in a few minutes," I said to Paige. "Cake at two."

Paige closed her history textbook. "I'm so happy that Eric made it. He deserved it."

"I know. And he's so excited. You sure you can't come and celebrate with us?"

"I would," Paige said. "But I already told Geena that I'd test recipes with her for cooking class."

"Okay." I gathered my books, highlighters, and pens to take back to my room. "See you later."

At the Sweet Shoppe, I spotted Andy, Troy, Ben, and Nicole at a table near the back. We chatted for a few minutes before Eric arrived.

"Ohhh, I see how it is," Nicole teased Eric. "You're a superstar rider now, so you can keep the rest of us waiting."

We all laughed.

"You got me," Eric said. "I knew you wouldn't eat the cake without me."

I dropped my jaw in mock-shock. "Puh-lease. I was about to go get it five seconds ago, but Troy stopped me."

Eric pretend-narrowed his eyes at me, but he couldn't stop his smile.

Andy checked the screen on his phone. "It's two ten," he said. "Jasmine still isn't here, so should we wait?"

"Yeah," Nicole said. "Like, ten more minutes. Then we eat."

"Let's get drinks," I said. Everyone agreed and soon, we were sipping our beverages of choice. I'd picked toasted almond–flavored iced coffee.

The guys had been talking about their last lesson.

"Did you have trouble with transitions?" Eric asked Troy and Ben.

Ben nodded and the guys kept talking.

Nicole scooted her chair closer to me. "I'm so happy that you and Eric are together," she said quietly. "You're great for each other."

"Thanks. I really, *really* like him."

"He's so into you," Nicole said. "It's obvious."

I played with my bracelet, touching the charm from Eric. "It'll be great to have him on my team too."

Nicole nodded, brushing back her curls. "For a while, anyway. You know you'll make the YENT, Sash."

"Ugh. Don't remind me about that. I can't even think about it now without hyperventilating."

"Don't." Nicole shook her head. "Or I'll send Rachel and her friends over to cheer for you when you ride."

That made me grin. "Exactly what I wanted."

We chatted for a few more minutes before Troy stood. "I'm going for the cake," he said. "We'll save Jas a couple of pieces."

Troy returned with a giant chocolate cake covered in whipped vanilla frosting. *Congratulations, Eric and Jasmine!* had been written across the center in hunter green icing—a Canterwood school color. Troy put the cake in the center of the table and Ben picked up a knife.

"Wait!" Nicole said. "We have to toast first."

"But . . . ," Ben said, staring longingly at the cake.

Nicole shot him a look and he put down the knife. Everyone picked up their drinks. "I think that since Sasha is already a member of the advanced team," Nicole said, winking at me, "she should toast Eric."

I shifted my coffee to the other hand. I was so proud of Eric that I could probably go on forever. "I never doubted that Eric would make the advanced team," I said. "I knew he would because he'd been working hard long before Mr. Conner invited him to try out."

Eric's smile encouraged me to keep going. "It's going to be amazing to have him as a teammate."

"But I hope we're not teammates for long," Eric interrupted.

I stared at him. "What?"

Eric reached over to touch my arm, smiling. "Because you're sure to ditch me for the YENT."

I laughed. "Ohhh. Well, yeah, then. I hope we're not teammates for long." I raised my cup. "To Eric and the advanced team."

"To Eric!" everyone else echoed. We touched our glasses together and I took a sip of my iced coffee.

Ben cut the cake and gave the first piece to Eric. Eric handed his plate to me.

"Enjoy, coach," he said. "I wouldn't have made it without you."

We all dug into the cake. Ben was practically licking crumbs off his plate when Jasmine stomped up to our table. She glared at us and shook her head.

"You guys are so rude," she snapped. "It's *barely* three."

"So . . . ?" I asked.

"Mr. Conner said to meet at three," Jasmine said. She folded her arms. "Nice of you to get here early to celebrate without me."

"We didn't," Andy said. "Mr. Conner said to get here at *two*."

Ben and Eric nodded.

"But don't worry," Nicole said. "We saved you some."

A look flashed over Jasmine's face. For a second, I thought it was sadness, but I wasn't sure. "Whatever. If you're done, just go already," Jas said. "I'd rather celebrate by myself anyway."

We stood and picked up our plates, leaving the cake for Jasmine. Outside the Sweet Shoppe, I turned to look back in the window. Jas sat by herself at the table, picking at a piece of cake with her fork. Her hair fell in front of her face and she made a halfhearted attempt to push it back.

When she thought no one was watching, I could tell she was lonely. I laced my fingers through Eric's, grateful all over again to have him and my friends.

16

FUN IN THE SUN

ON MONDAY, SPRING FEVER HIT CAMPUS. The temperature climbed into the low seventies and with a taste of summer in the air, no one could concentrate.

I squirmed though classes, eager to get outside. We only had a half day of classes because of some "staff development" workshop the teachers had to go to.

Morning lessons had been cancelled because the horses were getting vet checks, so my first advanced team lesson with Eric and Jasmine was this afternoon. I'd been thinking about it all morning.

"Sasha," Callie hissed, poking me in the ribs with a pen.

"What?" I looked up. Mr. Davidson was staring at me.

"C'mon, guys," Mr. Davidson said. "I know it's

gorgeous outside, but we've got to focus. Let's get back to the homework."

I forced myself to pay attention for the rest of class. Mr. Davidson dismissed us twenty minutes later and Callie and I gathered our papers and hurried down the hallway.

"Made it!" I cheered when we got outside.

"Let's do something outside," Callie said. "Our lesson isn't for a few hours. Want to take our books and go find a spot to hang out?"

"Yeah," I said. "I'll run back to Winchester and ask Paige if she wants to come and grab some towels. We could sit by the pasture and watch the horses while we work."

Callie nodded. "Love it."

Minutes later Paige, Callie and I met up at the knoll that overlooked the big pasture. Charm, Jack, Sunstruck, and Trix grazed together. The sunlight made Charm's coat gleam. Callie, Paige, and I put on our sunglasses and spread out the towels. We passed around my new coconut-flavored lip balm with sunscreen.

"This is the only way to study," Paige said as we sat down. We took our books out of our backpacks and I dug around until I found my favorite purple pen.

I looked back at the horses. "Aristocrat and Phoenix are missing."

Callie nodded, pulling a bag of cheddar Chex Mix out of her bag. "Heather and Jasmine are already riding." She opened the bag, poured some into her hand, and passed it to me. I grabbed a handful and gave the bag to Paige.

I felt a twinge of guilt that I wasn't working with Charm right now.

"Don't," Paige said, sliding her oval-shaped glasses down her nose to look at me. "You have to study too. Heather and Jasmine will be the ones crying when finals come around. We'll be ready."

"Right," I said. "I forgot how you have that thing where you read people's minds." I opened my bio book and turned to the chapter that Ms. Peterson had assigned.

I concentrated for a few minutes before my attention wandered and I ended up watching Charm graze. He looked gorgeous in the field.

"Today will be interesting, huh?" Callie asked. She capped her blue highlighter.

"Yeah, first lesson with Eric and Jas."

"At least you get to ride with your boyfriend," Callie said, laughing. "I'm still trying to get Jacob to pet Jack."

Paige stuck out her bottom lip. "Awww. I think it's kind of cute that he's scared of horses."

"It *is* cute," Callie said, twirling her pen in her fingers. "I like seeing that side of him."

"My boyfriend," Paige said. "can be scared of any animal he wants—I won't care. I just want one!"

We giggled.

"Oh, this is just great," someone said.

I turned and looked up at Heather, Julia, and Alison. Julia and Alison were in jeans and ballet flats, while Heather was in boots and breeches. Heather glared at me.

"What?" Callie asked.

"Oh, I don't know," Heather said, her blue eyes landing on Callie. "Maybe I'm just concerned that I'm the only one on *our* team who actually cares about the YENT."

"Why would you say that?" I asked.

Heather crossed her arms. "Silver, you're out here getting a tan. I'm actually *practicing* in the stable. And so is Jasmine."

"We're not 'tanning,'" Callie said. "We're studying. Grades count too, remember?"

"Oh, please," Julia snapped. "It's so not fair. You could be riding right now. Alison and I would be practicing every second if we could."

Alison just stood there, a half step behind Heather, looking out at the pasture and watching Sunstruck graze. The palomino gelding lifted his head and looked in our direction. He must have seen Alison, because he walked up to the fence and stuck his head over, reaching out his neck to her. Alison walked over and hugged his neck.

"Stop messing around," Heather said, her voice low. "This is our shot at the YENT, not Jasmine's. You'll both be sorry if you make this easy for her."

Julia and Heather stepped around our blankets and went over to Alison. The girls petted Sunstruck before walking away.

"You guys can go, if you want," Paige said. "We can study later."

I looked at Callie, then shook my head. "Nope," I said. "I'm staying. We have a lesson later and that's enough. I don't want to overpractice and burn Charm out."

"Agreed," Callie said. "We have homework to do."

17

STOP RADIATING
HEARTS ALREADY

THAT AFTERNOON AT THE STABLE, I RACED through tacking up Charm to get to the outdoor arena. I couldn't wait to have my first lesson with Eric. I'd worn my good breeches and had taken extra care to put on a shirt Charm hadn't stained. Luna's stall was empty, so Eric was probably warming up.

"You get to work out with Luna, boy," I said to Charm. "And I know you like her."

Charm bobbed his head and I laughed.

I hugged Charm before leading him down the aisle. Callie had Jack in crossties and was saddling him.

"Want me to wait for you?" I asked.

"No, go ahead," Callie said. "I'll be out in five."

I led Charm outside, mounted, and let him trot

toward the arena. Charm, loving the sun and warmer air, swished his tail. He had an extra bounce in his stride today.

As we entered the arena I saw that Eric and Heather were already inside. Heather circled Aristocrat at the far end and Eric trotted Luna along the fence. I urged Charm toward Luna and Eric stopped her when he saw me. Heather glanced at me, but kept riding.

"Hi," I said, pulling Charm up beside Luna.

"Hey, teammate," he said.

"Isn't it awesome?"

Eric nodded. "It's going to be great."

"This is *not* happening!" Heather said, huffing. She rode Aristocrat over to us and stopped him in front of Charm and Luna.

"What?" I asked.

Heather rolled her eyes. "You are so not doing boyfriend/girlfriend stuff during lessons. We're here to ride—not to make googly eyes at each other."

"We're not," I said, laughing. "You seriously need to be less crazy."

Eric just looked at Heather, an amused expression on his face.

Heather stared me down. "Save it, Silver. You're

practically radiating hearts. Just keep it out of the arena."

She spun Aristocrat around and cantered him away from us.

"Guess I better stay away from you," I said, looking at Eric.

He nodded with pretend seriousness. "You better. Stop radiating hearts already."

I was going to kill Heather later for saying that. I urged Charm in front of Luna. Jasmine came in a few minutes later and we all warmed up until Mr. Conner arrived.

"Good afternoon," Mr. Conner said, stopping in the center of the arena. Heather, Callie, Jasmine, Eric, and I halted our horses in front of him. "Since we have two new riders, ensuring a sense of teamwork is important. That's why, for today, we'll be doing drill team exercises."

Drill team? That meant—

"This means you'll all have to work together in unison," Mr. Conner said.

Jasmine looked over at me and shook her head.

"Don't drills usually need an even number of riders?" Callie asked.

"Yes," Mr. Conner said. "But there are a few drills that

work with an uneven number. Let's try one. Line up your horses at the end of the arena."

I was on the outside with Callie next to me, then Jasmine, Heather, and Eric. Mr. Conner stepped off to the side. "Walk your horses forward in a straight line and keep them even."

I asked Charm for a walk and he started forward, in step with Jack. Jasmine urged Phoenix at a faster walk and he jumped ahead of the other horses.

"Slower, Jasmine," Mr. Conner said.

Jasmine, frowning, pulled Phoenix back and got him in line. We managed to keep our horses together until we reached the end of the arena.

"Start back across at a trot," Mr. Conner instructed.

"Should we count?" Callie asked.

Jasmine rolled her eyes. "Do you *need* to count, Callie?"

"On three," Heather said, interrupting before Callie could respond. "One. Two. Three."

On three, the horses trotted. I eased Charm back when he started to nose in front of Jack. Charm's Thoroughbred blood was kicking in—he wanted to race! We trotted the horses down the arena and Eric and Luna fell back half a stride.

"Eric," Mr. Conner called. "Keep Luna moving."

Eric got Luna back in line with the rest of us.

"Can't you keep that slow horse moving?" Jasmine snapped at Eric.

Mr. Conner walked over before he could say anything.

"Good job," he said. "These exercises will teach you to work as a team and to pay attention to timing. Let's run through a few more."

Mr. Conner worked with us for another half hour before he dismissed us. "Nice work, everyone," he said. "See you next class."

He strode out of the arena and Heather rode Aristocrat beside Phoenix. "Are you *trying* to sink our team?" she asked Jasmine.

Jas rolled her eyes. "Do you think I care about the team? This drill stuff is so lame. Mr. Conner should be focusing on us as individuals so we have a better shot at the YENT."

Eric looked over at Jasmine. "We just spent forty-five minutes working on transitions and staying in control of our horses. Each of us—as *individuals*."

"Yeah," Callie added. "Mr. Conner knows what he's doing."

Jas sighed. "I don't even know how you made the team, Eric. But no big deal. I'll be off this team and onto the YENT soon anyway."

She trotted Phoenix away from us and I stared after her, tempted to chase her down and toss her into the big puddle by the fence.

Callie, Heather, Eric, and I just looked at each other. No words necessary.

18

CHEATING ON CHARM

"CHARM, IT'LL BE OKAY," I SAID. "WE'RE JUST going to play in the water."

It was a warm Saturday afternoon and I'd led Charm over to the creek to work on his water phobia. I'd texted Eric to see if he'd wanted to come, but he was playing baseball with his friends. Mr. Conner had said I could work with Charm at the part of the creek that was in sight of his office. He'd understood that I'd wanted to work through this on my own.

Charm snorted, slowing as we approached the creek. "C'mon," I said, patting his neck. "I'm right here."

I led him in small circles a few yards away from the creek bed. With every lap, I increased the size of the circle and led him closer to the creek. After ten minutes, I was dizzy and Charm was still feet away from the water.

"Let's go, boy," I said, leading him toward the creek. Here, the water was only six inches deep. But Charm dug in his heels, raising his head and refusing to step into the water. It wasn't like I could pull him in. I had to show Charm there was nothing to be afraid of.

I led Charm a couple of feet away from the creek and tied his lead line with a slip knot to a sturdy tree branch. Charm, relieved to be away from the water, relaxed and tipped his ears forward.

"Oh, we're not done," I said.

Charm watched as I walked away from him and stepped into the creek. I'd worn my pink rain boots so I could walk through the water. Water swirled around my ankles and I turned back to face Charm.

"See?" I asked him. "I'm totally fine."

Charm snorted like he didn't believe me. I stayed in the creek for a few minutes, sloshing my boots through the water. Charm kept his eyes on me the whole time. I finally untied him and patted his neck.

"Okay, that's it for today's water lesson. But next time, *you're* going in, 'kay?"

Charm and I walked back to the stable yard and I took him to the big pasture, turning him loose inside. "Later, boy." He trotted a few strides before breaking into a canter, his mane whipping through the air. He zoomed past Aristocrat and Phoenix and came to a halt beside Luna, who was grazing. Never shy about eating, Charm started munching grass beside her.

I turned and walked back to the stable to hang up his lead line. Inside, Alison had Sunstruck in crossties. The Arabian's coat gleamed. Alison had even polished his hooves.

"He looks amazing," I said.

Alison nodded. "Thanks. But he's bored. He loves to exercise and I haven't been able to do anything but lunge him."

I rubbed Sunstruck's cheek. "Can Heather ride him for you?"

"I asked her a few days ago," Alison said. "She will whenever she can."

"But she's probably superfocused on Aristocrat since the YENT tryouts are two and a half weeks away," I guessed.

Alison smoothed Sunstruck's mane. "Yeah."

"I could ride him sometime, if you want," I offered.

Alison looked up at me immediately. "Really? You would?"

"Sure," I said. "Charm's done for the day, so I'm free."

Alison smiled. "Thanks. Really. I was getting desperate."

"Desperate . . . awesome," I said, smiling back at her.

"You know what I mean. I'll go grab his tack." Alison darted off and came back with Sunstruck's gear and we tacked him up together. I got my helmet and changed into the spare pair of riding boots that I kept in my tack trunk. In the arena, Alison held him while I mounted. Sunstruck was a hand shorter than Charm and much slighter. For a second, I felt like I was cheating on Charm.

"Anything I should know?" I asked Alison, looking down at her.

"His mouth is sensitive," Alison said. "So keep your hands light. You've probably been around him enough to know everything else."

I nodded. "Okay. Let me get used to him, then you can coach us."

Alison moved into the center of the arena and I walked Sunstruck to the fence. He moved comfortably under me and I took him through a figure eight to get used to how he handled. He turned from the slightest movement of my hands.

"He's great," I told Alison.

"Thanks." She beamed. "Want to trot him?"

I nodded and let Sunstruck into a trot. His gait was smooth, almost like floating. Alison watched as we made two laps around the arena.

"Heels!" Alison called. I pushed down my heels.

"Cross over the center and reverse direction," Alison said.

I trotted Sunstruck past her and did a sitting trot around the arena. Alison coached us for a half hour before she finally nodded. "Ready to quit?" she asked.

I slowed Sunstruck to a walk and hopped off. "He's a great guy," I said, rubbing his neck. "I'm in love with Arabians now."

Alison laughed. I handed her the reins and unsnapped my helmet. "I'll take it back to the tack room," Alison offered.

"Thanks." I handed it to her. "And if you want me to ride him again, just ask."

"I will, thanks."

We looked at each other for a minute.

"Go ahead," Alison said. "Ask. You know you want to."

"If you guys *didn't* cheat, why does Drake keep saying there was evidence that you did?" I asked finally.

Alison looked me in the eye. "Jasmine."

"What? What does Jasmine have to do with anything?"

"I don't know why, but I just *know* she set us up somehow."

"But how?" I asked doubtfully.

Alison shook her head, staring at the ground.

"Have you told Heather that? You know she's looking for any excuse to take Jas down."

Alison nodded. "Don't say anything to anyone. Just forget about it."

Alison and I weren't friends, but I'd seen a different side to her before. My stomach turned in on itself. Suddenly, I had a sick, sinking feeling. What if Julia and Alison really were innocent?

19

HORSE OF A DIFFERENT COLOR

AFTER CLASSES ENDED FOR THE DAY, I dropped my books in my room and changed to go riding. Mr. Conner had a meeting with YENT scouts today, so he'd scheduled an extra practice for the advanced team this weekend. I eyed the pile of homework on my desk.

"It's growing," I said to Paige.

She nodded. "But you'll get it done. Only two more weeks of school before summer!"

"It seems so far away," I said. "But at least today's Sweet Shoppe day."

Paige nodded, her eyes widening. "Yeah. I think we each deserve *two* cupcakes today."

"Agreed."

When I got to the stable I found Eric by Luna's stall.

"Hi," I said.

"Hey," Eric said. "Feels like I never see you outside of the stable."

"No kidding. With finals coming up, homework, riding, and a zillion other things, it's been kind of crazy."

Eric reached out to take my hand. "Don't get too stressed out."

"I'll try not to," I said, concentrating on forming words. It was hard to talk to him when we held hands. "And to give us plenty of energy for homework, Paige and I are going to the Sweet Shoppe after I ride. Want to come?"

"Sure," Eric said.

"Be right back," I said. "I'm just going to grab Charm."

I walked down the aisle and stopped when I peered into Charm's stall. It was empty.

Not. Happening. Again. Hiding horses was so last semester!

I spun around and almost slammed into Jasmine.

"Watch it, Sasha," Jasmine said, shaking her head. "You could hurt someone."

"Where's Charm?" I asked. "Did you move him? If you did anything to him, I'll—"

Jasmine held up a hand. "Calm down. Poor Charm looked bored in his stall, so I turned him out in the back pasture."

"What? Why?" I asked. "Why would you move *my* horse when you knew I was coming to ride?"

Jasmine pouted. "I'm sorry. I thought I was doing something nice for him. And since you're not so serious about the team, I figured there'd be a chance that you'd skip riding."

"That's ridiculous," I argued. "Whatever. I'm going to get Charm."

I stepped away from Jas and took a side exit, heading for the back pasture. *Charm's hooves are going to be sooo muddy,* I thought, thinking about the downpour earlier today. It was going to take me at least twenty minutes to get them clean. I stopped midstep.

My horse wasn't a chestnut anymore. He'd turned bay! Charm was coated from forelock to tail in mud. A *thick* coat of mud.

Jasmine.

Was.

Dead.

"Charm!" I said.

Charm trotted up to me and bumped my arm with his muzzle, streaking mud on my jacket sleeve.

"Hey!" I cried. But Charm blinked innocently. He loved it.

I grasped his mud-coated halter and led him out of the pasture and into the stable.

As he walked down the aisle, mud splattered onto the floor. Eric's back was to me as he cleaned Luna's hoof.

"Help!" I wailed.

Eric looked up and almost dropped Luna's leg. He set it down and stared, shaking his head. "What happened?"

"Jasmine! She turned Charm out and did this to him. I'm going to find her and—"

Eric stepped away from Luna. "She just left. Forget her—focus on Charm. Want my help washing him?"

"If you want," I said. "But you totally don't have to."

"I don't mind," Eric said. "We'll finish faster together and then we can go riding."

We walked Charm to the outdoor wash stall. Eric clipped him into the crossties and I filled a bucket with warm water and Mane 'n' Tail shampoo. I turned the hose on low and aimed it at Charm's hooves. I moved it up his legs, then his chest, and finally let water run down his back.

Charm didn't move. "You love a bath, but you won't go through the creek?" I asked him.

Eric grabbed a rubber currycomb and started loosening the mud clumps on Charm's forelegs. "How's that going?"

"Not well," I admitted. "I've been in the water more

than he has. But I'm going to get him over it before the YENT. I have to."

"You will. And I'll help you whenever I can."

"That would be great." I moved the hose over Charm's back, trying to rinse away as much mud as possible before I started scrubbing. Water ran down Charm's hindquarters, sending streams of dirty water down his tail and onto the rubber mats under him. I put down the hose and picked up a soapy sponge.

"At least I can see Chestnut now," I said. "Before he was—ahhh!"

I shrieked when Charm swished his tail, slapping me in the chest and face. Globs of mud stuck to my jacket and I swiped at dirt on my face. "CHARM!"

Eric, crouched by Charm's left foreleg, stood and peered around Charm at me. "Oh, Sasha. You . . ." He smirked and his shoulders started to shake.

"Eric!" I said, glancing down at my muddy jacket. "It's not funny!"

"I know!" Eric said. "I'm sorry, but . . ." He couldn't finish his sentence. He burst into laughter and walked over to me, grabbing me in a hug. Within seconds, I was laughing too. When he let me go, he had mud smudged on his gray shirt.

I ran my hand along Charm's barrel, coating my fingers with mud. "This," I said. "is for laughing at me!"

I wiped my hand on the side of Eric's face and left a giant streak of mud.

"Sasha Silver!" Eric boomed.

I giggled. "Now we match!"

"Oh, yeah?" Eric grabbed the hose and held it, pointing the nozzle at me and daring me to move.

"You wouldn't," I said, taking a step backward. Charm looked at me as if to say, *Don't even try to use me as a shield.*

Eric stepped forward and kept the hose aimed at me. "Oh, I think I would."

"But! But!" I protested, laughing. "I'm your girlfriend. You can't hose your girlfriend. It's, like, a rule."

Eric rolled his eyes to the sky, as though thinking. "Really? Never heard it."

"Eriiiic," I said. "Don't—"

A stream of cold water hit me in the chest and I screamed. "Ahhhhh! Omigod! Eric!"

I reached down and grabbed the bucket of dirty water, sloshing it in Eric's direction. He started to dart away from me and I soaked his back. Eric stopped and turned slowly, his hair dripping. He kept the hose trained on me.

I was out of ammo.

"Truce?" I begged.

Eric stared at me for what felt like forever before lowering the hose. "Truce."

We collapsed into laughter near the grass beside the wash stall with Charm—the only clean one of the three of us—looking over us.

20

AWKWARD

LATER THAT AFTERNOON PAIGE AND I WENT to the Sweet Shoppe together to meet Eric. We walked inside and looked for an empty table. At a booth near the back, Callie and Jacob had their heads bent together over an ice cream sundae. Callie, seeing us, waved. Jacob glanced up and nodded once before focusing back on the ice cream.

Why couldn't he just stop being awkward around me?!

Paige and I sat at a table near the window.

"He can't even look at you," Paige whispered.

"I know. One second, he acts like we have a shot at being friends again and the next, he won't even talk to me. I don't get it."

Paige played with her menu. "Maybe he just doesn't know how to be friends. He——"

I shot Paige the *zip-it!* eyes when Eric walked in. I didn't want him to hear us talking about Jacob. That would only result in more awkwardness.

"Hey," he said sitting across from me. "You look a lot cleaner."

"Ha, ha," I said. "I told Paige what you did."

Paige shook her head, teasingly. "Not cool, Eric."

"But did Sasha tell you what *she* did to me?" Eric asked.

Paige peered at me. "Sasha?"

I tried not to look guilty. "I *might* have put a tiny bit of mud on Eric's face."

Eric's brown eyes focused on me. "Tell the truth, Sash."

"Oh, fine! I swiped an entire handful of mud on his face."

Paige giggled. "You conveniently left that part out."

I shrugged and we all cracked up.

"Let's order," Eric said, after we'd calmed down. "What do you guys want?"

I didn't have to think about my order. "I'll have chocolate pudding and a Coke," I said.

"Sticking with the theme of the day, huh?" Eric asked.

I nodded. "Yep. The pudding will remind me of how I got you."

He mock-rolled his eyes. "Paige?"

"Ooooh, mint chocolate pudding for me, and a Coke too, please," Paige said.

We handed Eric our student ID cards to charge the food to our accounts.

Callie and Jacob got up from their table and walked by. "See you, guys," Callie said to Paige and me.

"Bye," we said.

Eric, waiting for our orders at the counter, turned and saw Callie and Jacob. He gave Callie a quick smile and eyed Jacob. Jacob glared back and almost stopped walking until Callie shot him a look. Eric watched Jacob until the door shut behind them. When he put our snacks and drinks on the table, he was still frowning.

I wanted to tell him that he didn't have to get annoyed every time he saw Jacob, but I didn't say anything.

"Probably one of our last afternoons of fun before we have to start crazy studying," Paige said.

"I'm starting tonight," I said. "Good-bye, TV and movies."

Eric sipped his soda. "I'm getting the impression that finals are tough here."

Paige nodded. "They're hard, but you just have to study. A lot. Oh, and don't sleep. Just . . . study. Constantly."

Eric lowered his spoon into his bowl of chocolate ice cream. "You're kidding, right?"

"Not really," Paige said, hanging her head. "You'll see."

We joked about finals and chatted till we'd all finished our snacks.

"I've got to go," Eric said. "I told Troy I'd meet him."

He squeezed my hand before getting up. "Text you later."

"Okay. Bye." I smiled at him.

Paige and I looked at each other.

"Do we *have* to go study?" I asked.

"After I have one more sip," Paige said. She started to take a drink, but her eyes stopped on something over my shoulder. Her face turned the same color as her pink straw and she coughed, almost sputtering soda.

"Paige?" I leaned toward her. "Are you okay?"

"Yes," she squeaked. She put down her soda and looked at the table. Paige pulled the menu in front of her and started reading it.

"Aren't we leaving? What happened?" I looked behind me.

Ryan, an incredibly cute guy from Paige's math class, stood at the counter. He'd also played a security guard at her *Teen Cuisine* premiere party.

"Omigod," I whispered. "You like Ryan!"

Paige picked up the menu and shielded her face.

"Paige!" I reached over and pulled down the menu.

Paige inched down into the booth. "Yes," she whispered. "I like him. But I can't talk to him right now. I don't know what to say."

"He hasn't seen you. Don't worry." I glanced over my shoulder again, pretending to look at the wall clock. The barista handed Ryan a soda and he walked out the door.

"Phew," Paige said. "Let's go in case he comes back."

It was so funny to see Paige act this way! She was usually so calm and supercomposed. I'd never seen her this flustered.

We got up and walked to the door. Paige checked out the window to be sure Ryan had walked away before we went outside.

"You should totally talk to him," I said. "He was into you at your party. I know it."

Paige's eyes widened. "You think?"

"I know."

21

OWNED!

"TODAY'S GOING TO BE <u>AWESOME</u>," I SAID. "Cross-country!" I peered out the window of our room, overlooking the sidewalks and lawn. A gentle breeze swayed the trees and puffy clouds filled the sky.

Paige, looking up from her homework, nodded. "Your fave. And tonight . . ."

I pretended to think. "Something's on tonight. Let me think . . . Friday night . . . there's a show on Friday night . . . some show with a girl and there might be, like, cooking."

Paige tossed a wadded up piece of notebook paper at me. "Meet me in the common room for snacks and stuff."

I pulled on my boots. "I'll be there."

*

At the stable yard I mounted Charm as Callie led Jack toward us. Callie looked like a riding catalog model—she wore a royal purple three-quarter-sleeve shirt, black breeches, and matching cross-country vest.

"I'm so psyched for cross-country!" Callie said.

"Me too," I said. "I'm ready."

"Ready to get owned at cross-country?" I asked Eric with a teasing smile when he and the rest of the team finally arrived.

"Oh, please," Eric said. "You're good, but not that good."

I folded my arms. "Excuse me? I'm so gonna take you down for that."

Eric just shook his head.

"*That's* new," I heard Heather say. I followed her gaze. *Mr. Conner* was on horseback. He trotted Brooklyn, a gelding he was training, over to us. I wasn't used to seeing him on horseback during our lessons.

Mr. Conner let Brooklyn trot past us, and then looked back over his shoulder. "C'mon. Let's go!"

The rest of us urged our horses after Mr. Conner and we let them trot across the field to the start of the course.

"One at a time on the course," Mr. Conner said. "Heather will go first, then Eric, Jasmine, Sasha, and Callie. After the rider in front of you goes, wait five minutes before you start. Pay attention to the course flags. If you get into trouble, remember that someone will be a few minutes behind you."

We nodded.

"And Callie," Mr. Conner said. "If we don't see you within ten minutes after Sasha comes in, I'll be on the course."

I rubbed Charm's neck and he snorted. Neither of us could wait to get out there.

"Like last time, I'm going to take a shortcut across the field. I'll be waiting at the finish line," Mr. Conner said.

Mr. Conner cantered Brooklyn away from us and Heather circled Aristocrat.

"Try not to end up in the creek, Heather," Jasmine said.

Heather turned in her saddle and glared at Jasmine before settling into Aristocrat's saddle. Finally, she asked him to canter. Aristocrat's long strides carried them to the stone wall. Aristocrat jumped the wall and he and Heather disappeared into the woods.

A few minutes later, Eric adjusted his cross-country vest and started out.

"Good luck," I said.

"Gag," Jasmine said, rolling her eyes. "Would you just go already?"

Eric tapped his heels against Luna's sides and she quickly accelerated into a canter. Her strides were shorter than Aristocrat's, but she was fast. Eric guided her to the wall and she took it without hesitation.

Jasmine rode off a few minutes later, then it was finally my turn.

"Have fun," Callie said. "And don't even worry about the creek. Remember, you can jump the skinniest part on this course."

I nodded and sank my weight into the saddle.

"Ready, boy?" I gave Charm rein and urged him forward. He cantered across the field and we reached the low stone wall with ivy growing along the top and sides. Charm lifted into the air and tucked his forelegs under his body. We landed on the other side and I let him canter for a few dozen yards down the straight dirt path.

I slowed Charm as we approached a log pile. Charm leaped the logs and he cantered for six strides before we made a gradual turn and started toward the creek. I tried not to tense in the saddle, but I was nervous. I took a breath and paid attention to Charm's body language—waiting for a flicker of nerves from him. But his canter didn't slow as we approached the creek. I started counting strides. *Four, three, two, one, and up!* I squeezed my legs against Charm's sides and he pushed with his hind legs, propelling us over the creek. I let out a breath when we landed on the dirt bank on the other side.

"Nice," I said as we trotted uphill and then through the final yards of woods. Charm's canter quickened as the dirt changed to grass. Four jumps left. We trotted up another hill and the ground leveled. I could see Eric, Heather, and Jasmine waiting with Mr. Conner.

I aimed Charm at a stack of hay bales and he jumped them without blinking. He took two brush jumps, with only a couple of strides between them, and then moved toward the final jump—a wooden gate. Charm tossed his head, tugging on the reins. He wanted to stretch into a gallop over the final yards toward the gate.

Not. Happening.

I squeezed the reins with my fingers, deepening my seat and lengthening my legs. Charm cantered a few more strides at the same speed before slowing.

Three, two, one, and up! I lifted out of the saddle and Charm jumped with too much force over the old brown gate. He jumped higher than necessary, landing heavily on the other side. My hands slid down his neck and I wobbled in the saddle. Gripping the saddle with my knees, I corrected my seat.

I slowed Charm to a trot, then a walk. Mr. Conner rode Brooklyn up to us.

"How did it go?" he asked.

"I was nervous before the creek," I admitted. "But Charm didn't have a problem jumping it."

"You did the right thing by doing a half halt to slow him before the gate," Mr. Conner said. "He saw the other horses waiting and wanted to rush to get to them."

"He still jumped too high," I said. "But I shouldn't have lost my balance."

Mr. Conner nodded. "We'll work on balance exercises before tryouts."

When we joined the others, Charm stopped by Luna and reached out his muzzle to bump hers.

"Good ride?" Eric asked.

"Decent," I said. "Not our best. But at least now I know what to work on."

"Everything," Jas quipped under her breath.

I rolled my eyes, but I was really worried. I couldn't make those mistakes during the final YENT tryouts. While we waited for Callie, I tried not to obsess over my ride. Callie and Jack finally appeared over the hill and I watched Jack fly over the gate with ease that I envied. It only made me more nervous about tryouts.

Going into film class, I was still thinking about my cross-country mistakes.

As I took my seat, I flipped open my phone to find that Callie had sent me a text.

Meet me aftr class?

K.

She'd promised to help me in whatever way she could so that we'd both be as prepared as possible for the try-outs. I put my phone away, glad for the millionth time to have my BFF back.

Mr. Ramirez walked to the front of the room. "Happy Friday, everyone."

What movie was that from?! We looked around at each other—no one knew!

Mr. Ramirez stared at us for a few more seconds before starting to laugh. "That wasn't a quote, guys. I was really just saying 'happy Friday.'"

I laughed along with the rest of the class.

"Please pass your homework forward," Mr. Ramirez said. "And then we'll get started."

Where was Jacob? His knee was fine—Callie had said so earlier today. I reached for my phone, then changed my mind.

"Anyone have problems with the homework?" Mr. Ramirez asked.

A girl in the front row raised her hand. "Question three?"

"Okay," Mr. Ramirez said, collecting the homework. "Let's take a look at question three." Mr. Ramirez stopped, his gaze focused on something else.

"Sorry," Jacob said, hurrying down the aisle and taking the seat next to me.

Mr. Ramirez frowned. "I know it's the last day of class, guys, but we still have work to do today. Let's go back to Alicia's question."

When Mr. Ramirez started talking, I leaned over to Jacob. "You okay?"

He nodded.

I looked at him. He kept shifting around in his seat and touching his hair, which I knew he did when he got nervous. I wanted to ask him if he was really okay, but decided to drop it. If he wanted to talk, he would.

At the end of class, Mr. Ramirez told us that he had one last announcement. "Since I'm the nicest teacher at

Canterwood," he said, "you all already know there's no final for this class. But the powers that be have insisted on something official in place of an exam. So instead, we'll be having a class pizza party on Saturday afternoon." Mr. Ramirez grinned. "We'll watch a couple of my favorite movies and that will be that. It was either that or a final, so I hope you're all on board."

"Um, yeah!" called a guy two rows in front of me.

Everyone laughed and Mr. Ramirez dismissed us. Jacob gathered his bag and immediately walked down the aisle to Mr. Ramirez, probably to explain why he'd been late.

When I walked out of the theater, I found Callie waiting for me. She'd pulled her hair into a high ponytail that showed off her pink dangly earrings.

"How was class?" she asked.

"Long, but okay. I can't believe it was the last one." We started to walk and then I paused. "Did you want to wait for Jacob?" I asked.

Callie shook her head and took a seat on a couch near the back of the common room. "Nope. He's going to text me later."

I dropped my bag on the ground and rifled through it till I found my notebook. "I started making a list of everything I need to fix before the YENT tryouts," I said, flipping to the right page and handing the notebook to Callie.

Callie's eyes scanned my notes. She glanced back at me, folding her legs under her.

"Sash, this is a great list. But . . . you can't be a *perfect* rider. No one can. We can all try to improve on these things, but you'll never be a flawless rider."

I held out my hand for the notebook. I looked at my list again. "Deeper seat, better extension, no rushing jumps, no fear of water, less tension from me." I stopped reading. "You don't think I can fix all of those things in a week and a half?"

Callie nodded and scooted closer to me. "Of course! Improve—absolutely. But trying to make sure your ride is totally perfect? None of us can do that. I think you're putting a lot of pressure on yourself. It could make try-outs even harder if you're worried about a list this long."

"Maybe." I blew out a breath. "But I still want to do everything I can to have the best possible ride. Aren't you worried too?"

"I'd be crazy if I wasn't!" Callie said. "But just try not to stress too much."

I started to pause for a second, thinking about how un-Callie-like she sounded. Callie, always the champion of hard work, was telling *me* not to worry? Usually, it was the other way around. But maybe Callie was grasping that ever elusive balance between riding, school, boys, and friends—something I still hadn't found.

"You're right." I tore my page out of my notebook and crumpled it. "I don't need a list to tell me what to do," I said. "Charm and I will be ready."

"Exactly," Callie said. "No more obsessing about try-outs today. What are you up to tonight?"

I put away my notebook. "Nothing," I said. "Just . . . oh, no!" I jumped up off the couch and grabbed my bag.

"What?" Callie looked up at me, her brown eyes wide.

I smacked my forehead. "I was supposed to meet Paige right after class to watch *Teen Cuisine*. I'm late!" I started toward the door. "Wanna come?"

"Absolutely!"

I picked up the crumpled list and dropped it in the trash as we left the media center. Callie was right—I knew what I needed to do.

22

TEAMWORK
TRAIN WRECK

BY TUESDAY ALMOST EVERYONE ON CAMPUS
was in crazy mode. Finals started next Monday and the
teachers had kicked reviewing into overdrive. I walked into
bio class and sat down. Julia and Alison, who'd been whispering when I'd walked in, turned to look at me.

"How's practice?" Alison asked. Usually, this would
have felt like a trap. But she looked genuinely curious.

I made a noncommittal so-so motion with my hand.
"Okay. I'm just ready to get tryouts over with."

Julia shook her head. "At least you *have* a shot."

As Jasmine entered the room, she took one look at my
face and shook her head.

"Wow," Jasmine said. "Sasha, the YENT tryouts
aren't even here yet and you look superstressed—

the dark under-eye circles look good on you."

I focused on the whiteboard in front of me. *She's not worth it,* I repeated to myself. But as evil as she was, could she really pull off framing Julia and Alison?

"Turn to page one-seventy and we'll get started," Ms. Peterson said.

As Ms. Peterson continued with the lesson, I forced myself to take notes and reminded myself what Callie had said. I couldn't let Jas's trash talk mess with my head.

At our afternoon lesson, Jas was even worse. She smirked every time she looked at me and kept rolling her eyes at Eric.

"Sasha, please pay attention," Mr. Conner called out. "I know we're getting close to tryouts and that's exciting, but I need everyone to focus."

I blushed and nodded.

"Now that your horses are warmed up, let's run through a few drill exercises," Mr. Conner said.

Next to me, Jasmine sighed quietly.

"I want you to line up your horses one behind the other with a few strides between them. This is called a 'nose to tail' exercise. We'll start with lots of space between each horse then gradually decrease it."

Heather lined up first, then Jasmine, Eric, Callie, and I. We looked to Mr. Conner for instructions.

"Walk to the halfway point of the arena, then trot," he said.

Heather started and we followed behind her. Everyone kept their horses at the right distance and when she reached the halfway point of the arena, Heather urged Aristocrat into a trot. Jasmine and Eric followed, maintaining the space between them. Charm trotted behind Jack and worked to keep his speed even.

As we started the turn, Callie let Jack slow down. It shortened the distance between Charm and Jack.

"Watch the pacing, Callie," Mr. Conner said. "Everyone needs to maintain the same distance between their horses."

Mr. Conner made us do the nose to tail exercise at a walk, trot, and finally a canter. At a canter, it was challenging to pay attention to Charm *and* the horse in front of me. Mr. Conner kept switching up our riding order and I made sure I was even more focused when Jasmine was behind me.

"Great work, everyone," Mr. Conner said, a half hour later. "We'll stop here for today. Please cool your horses and I'll see you tomorrow morning."

We dismounted and led the horses in lazy circles around the arena. Eric and I cooled out Charm and Luna in comfortable silence.

"Biggest mystery ever?" Jasmine asked. "Why you even bother coming to lessons at all. You know *I'm* the only one who's going to make the YENT. Such a waste of—"

"Shut *up!*" Heather hissed. Both girls halted their horses.

Jas cocked her head and placed a hand on her hip. "You did *not* just say that."

"The trash talk is getting old," Heather said. "If I hear one more word about how you're the best rider on campus and how awful the rest of us are, we're going to have a serious problem." Heather's eyes stayed locked on Jasmine.

Jas snorted. "Oh, Heather. You think you're such a great rider. Heather Fox, Queen Bee of Canterwood. Puh-lease. I've got news for you. You're generic, at best. And also? I'll say anything I want. If it makes you that insecure, then bonus."

Heather looked as though she might leap over and pounce on the dark-haired girl. She made a face like she'd swallowed sour milk and gritted her teeth.

"*I'm* insecure?" Heather seethed.

"Clearly."

Heather fake smiled, flashing her teeth. "The only thing that's *clear* is that you have a choice to make. Either stop trying to mess with *my* team, or, I'll—"

"You'll what?" Jas interrupted. She walked Phoenix closer to Aristocrat. "I don't think I need to remind you who my friends are."

Heather laughed and smoothed back her hair. "Like I care about the Belles. The second they drop you—and they will—you're going to be sorry you ever showed your face at Canterwood."

I couldn't stop watching. It was a total train wreck—and even though I'd been on the receiving end of Heather's fierce reamings more than once, I wasn't sad to watch Jasmine squirm. In fact, I was pretty much loving it. Jasmine took vicious to a whole other level. With a twinge, I thought once again about my conversation with Alison. I'd witnessed firsthand the non–study habits of Julia and Alison. I'd been with them on more than one occasion when they chose texting over cracking even one book. But would they cheat? I wasn't so sure.

Jasmine, obviously having had enough, pulled Phoenix forward and led him out of the arena.

Callie and I traded looks—this incident would clearly require several hours of discussion.

"Sweet Shoppe?" I whispered to Callie.

"Given," she said.

I led Charm over to Luna. Eric loosened her girth another notch and smiled when he saw me.

"Callie and I are going to the Sweet Shoppe after this," I said.

"Cool," Eric said. "Text you later."

"Sounds good," I said.

Callie and I groomed Jack and Charm and washed up in the Sweet Shoppe bathroom afterward. I watched as Callie expertly applied a layer of shiny pink gloss.

"You didn't used to be so into makeup," I said.

Callie glanced at me. "Yeah. I guess I didn't. But I like it now."

Because of Jacob, I almost said. But I knew that would have been the wrong thing to say.

We walked out by the counter and scanned the rows of treats behind the glass.

"I'm feeling donuts," I said.

"Me too," Callie agreed. "Glazed *and* chocolate."

"And that's why we're friends," I said, giggling.

Minutes later, we were eating donuts and sipping pink lemonade at a corner table. I noticed that Callie's eyes were glued to the tabletop.

"What's up?" I asked. "You okay?"

Callie picked at her donut and finally glanced up at me. "There's so much going on right now," she said.

"You mean with riding and finals?" I asked.

"Yeah," she said. "And everything else."

I put down my glass. "Everything else?"

"Jacob, I guess. I want to do things with him, too, but we're both so busy. Riding takes up so much time. I mean, I love it, but I also wish we had more time to hang out before summer."

"I get why you feel that way," I said. "But Jacob understands. He knows this is a huge opportunity. And things aren't always going to be like this—you're not going to be practicing for the YENT forever."

Callie nodded. "True," she said. But she didn't seem convinced.

23

SO BEYOND PIZZA PARTY

ON SATURDAY MORNING, ERIC AND I MET UP for breakfast at the caf. He'd taken my order and brought us both plates of steaming hot blueberry waffles with whipped cream and giant glasses of OJ. He put down our plates and sat across from me.

"It's like our last meal," I teased. "The last weekend before finals."

Eric groaned. "Don't remind me." He took a bite of waffle. "I'm trying to forget the fact that we're about to go to the library to study for endless hours."

I ate a forkful of whipped cream. "And I'll probably be there tomorrow too. And every day until Friday. But then . . ."

"It's over," Eric finished. "You'll be trying out and

making the YENT. And I'll be there cheering you on."

After breakfast, we went to the library and piled our books on top of a corner table and started studying. Eric quizzed me for bio and then it was my turn to test him on every detail about William Shakespeare.

"Date of birth?" I asked.

"1564," Eric said.

"Married to . . ."

"Anne Hathaway," Eric answered without pausing.

I flipped to another page. "Those were too easy. Let me find a hard question." I scanned Eric's notes. "Okay. Name three plays." I held up a finger. "*Not* including *Hamlet*."

Eric shook his head. "You call that a challenge? *Twelfth Night*. *Othello*. And . . ." he paused.

"And?" I prompted.

Eric's eyes went to the ceiling. "*King Lear!*" he said finally.

We studied together for a couple of more hours before my brain went fuzzy. "I'm done," I said. "Brain. Hurts."

"Mine too." Eric closed his book.

"Just in time for my last film class. Mr. Ramirez is showing a couple of his favorite movies."

"Oh, right," Eric said. "Weird that he's doing that on a Saturday."

I paused. Should I tell him it was a party and Jacob would be there?

"Well," I said. "It's instead of a final, remember?"

"Oh, that's cool," Eric said.

I pulled my strawberry banana Lip Smacker out of my purse and applied some. "Yeah, and . . . it's a pizza party."

"Fun," Eric said. He stuffed his books into his bag. "Way better than a final, that's for sure. See you later?"

"'Kay," I said. "See you later."

I peered at my reflection one last time before heading to film. I'd picked out a summery white skirt, a pink tank, and white zip cardigan with silver sandals. I ran my fingers through my flatironed hair and fastened my small, silver hoop earrings.

Paige smiled when she saw me. "Wow. You look amazing. That outfit is so beyond pizza party."

I frowned and looked in the mirror again. "It is?"

Paige nodded and sat on her bed. "In the best possible way!"

I picked up my purse and dropped my phone inside. "Thanks. I'll see you later."

"Wait," Paige said. She ran over to my desk and picked up my charm bracelet. "Want this?"

"Definitely. I can't believe I forgot it." Paige fastened the bracelet to my wrist.

I walked down the hallway, shaking my head. I'd *never* forgotten that bracelet. Especially not since Eric had given me my new charm.

The common room door opened and Jasmine walked out into the hallway. She stopped, staring at me.

"Date with Eric?" she asked, sounding bored.

"Maybe." Like I was going to explain to her where I was going.

"Because you need to be aware of how dressy-slash-hideous those clothes are," Jasmine said. "Poor Eric."

"Whatever." I brushed past her and walked outside. On my way to the media center, someone familiar walked a few feet in front of me.

"Jacob?" I called.

But he didn't turn around. I hurried to catch up. "Jacob?" I called again. This time he stopped.

"Oh, hey," he said. His gaze was friendly and he stuck his hands in the pockets of his jeans.

Neither of us looked at each other as we walked.

"I'm kind of sad this class is over," I said. "Are you?"

Jacob nodded. "Me too. Mr. R. is a cool guy."

I wished it could just be like this—friendly and not weird

the way it had been. I couldn't help but smile at him.

When we got to the media center, he pulled open the door for me and we went into the theater together. The scent of pizza filled the theater.

"Mmmm," I said. "Pepperoni."

Jacob grinned and sniffed. "And Hawaiian."

Mr. Ramirez had a table set up along the wall and pizza boxes lined the tabletop. Jacob and I grabbed paper plates and I piled mine with three slices of pepperoni. We grabbed cups of soda and started toward our seats.

"Oh," I said, stopping before I started down our row. "I guess we don't have to sit together anymore."

Jacob shrugged. "I'm sitting in my old seat."

"Okay," I said, following him. "Me too."

We took our seats and started eating while Mr. Ramirez set up the film. I glanced at Jacob a couple of times. Something had changed. He'd shifted away from me and wasn't talking anymore.

The theater darkened and I took another bite of pizza. The movie, a comedy I'd never heard of, was hilarious and in five minutes, Jacob and I were laughing. I almost spilled my soda on my skirt and Jacob caught my eye and made me laugh harder. After the movie ended, Mr. Ramirez played a half-hour documentary about aspiring young filmmakers.

"I'm glad I took film," I said to Jacob as the credits rolled.

"Me too. I'll be quoting film lines all of the time now," he said.

I looked at Jacob, pausing. I was sad that the class was over, but there was something else too, something I couldn't quite put my finger on.

"I hope everyone had fun tonight," Mr. Ramirez said from the front of the class, pushing up his glasses. "Because I've truly enjoyed having you all in my class. Even if you never take another film class, it's my hope that you'll look at movies with a new appreciation."

I nodded. That was a given.

"If you'd all come up to the table beside me, I have something for each of you."

Jacob and I were among the first ones at the table. Mr. Ramirez reached into a black box and pulled out a DVD case. "Here, Sasha. Thank you for taking my class."

I took the plastic case from him and looked at it. Mr. Ramirez handed the next one to Jacob. *Horse Sense by Sasha Silver and Jacob Schwartz* was typed on a DVD jacket. I opened the case and a disc was inside. Mr. Ramirez had made us all copies of our student films.

"Wow!" I said. "Thank you so much."

He smiled. "I want you all to be proud of your films and keep working on your talents."

"Jacob, isn't this—" But I stopped short when I saw that no one was next to me. Jacob was already gone.

24

DID THEY OR DIDN'T THEY?

BY SEVEN THIRTY ON MONDAY MORNING,
Paige and I had been up and studying for hours. Our room looked like Office Depot. Pens, highlighters, notebooks, and paper clips were everywhere. My math final was today and Paige had English.

"We've got this, right?" I asked. I started to rub my face with my hand until I saw the pen marks and highlighter streaks on it.

"Totally," Paige said. "We'll do great. And we'll keep counting them down till Friday."

We gathered our things and left for class. When I took my seat in the classroom, I took a shaky breath and gripped my pen with sweaty fingers. Ms. Utz, my math teacher and guidance counselor, passed out testing booklets. She towered over the class—all six feet of her.

I smiled at the memory of the first time I'd heard about Ms. Utz and her championship wrestling career. Jacob had told me. That day in Utz's office was the first time I'd ever spoken to him. His warnings about Utz had made me less nervous about deciding my schedule.

And I'd given a similar warning to Eric when he'd transferred to Canterwood this semester.

"Does everyone have a test?" Ms. Utz asked.

We nodded. I turned on my calculator and sat up straighter.

"Then you may begin," she said.

I opened the test booklet and started solving for x.

After school I changed into my riding clothes and started toward the stable. Afternoon riding lessons were never mandatory during midterms or finals, but Mr. Conner had to know that none of us trying out for the YENT would take a break.

I texted Callie. *Made it thru final. U?*

Me 2. Won't b @ stbl 4 1 hr.

C u then.

I texted Eric next. *U riding now?*

Can't. Got paper 2 write.

Good luck!

I grabbed Charm's tack and saw Alison and Julia grooming Trix and Sunstruck in the aisle. Julia's short blond hair was pushed back with a skinny plastic headband—something she'd never be able to wear if she was riding.

"Hey," I said. "How's it going?"

Julia rolled her eyes. "How do you *think* it's going? We're stuck missing the YENT tryouts because of something we didn't do. So, *Sasha,* not so great."

"Sorry," I said. "I was just asking."

Alison flicked a purple body brush over Sunstruck's shoulder. "It's just a little hard to watch you, Callie, Heather, and Jas get ready for the YENT when we can't."

"If you really didn't do it, I'm sure you'll find some way to get back on the team," I said.

"Are you going to talk to us all day or are you actually going to ride?" Julia snapped.

Alison shot me an *I'm sorry* look behind Julia's back.

I walked away from them and tacked up Charm. I hugged him before I got into the saddle, taking in his sweet scent of hay and grain.

"I'm really, really nervous about tryouts," I whispered to him. "You think we can do it?"

Charm looked at me, then rubbed his head on my arm, leaving white hairs on my blue sleeve.

"Thanks," I said, rolling my eyes. "My shirt needed something extra."

I started to lead Charm toward the outdoor arena, then changed my mind. I turned him and we went to the smaller back arena instead. I warmed Charm up by walking and trotting him around the arena for a few minutes before starting figure eights. I maneuvered him through the pattern and then switched to spirals. Charm moved well under me and it made me a little less nervous about Saturday.

Callie and Jack walked around the side of the stable and Callie waved at me. She mounted and I stopped Charm so we could talk.

"Did you see Heather on your way over here?" Callie asked.

"No. Why?"

"I saw her a minute ago," Callie said. "She was on the phone and holding Aristocrat. She looked really upset."

Her dad, I thought.

"Julia and Alison are in the stable," I said. "I'm sure she'll talk to them if something's up."

"Right. You ready to work?" Jack shifted under Callie and pawed the dirt.

"Ready. Let's do it." We let the horses trot and spent an hour working them through different patterns.

"Do you think Julia and Alison will find a way to make it to YENT tryouts?" I asked Callie when we stopped for a break.

"I don't know. They've worked so hard—I hope so. But it doesn't seem likely. They'd have to prove they didn't cheat."

I still wasn't sure. But the more I talked to Alison, the more I thought they might be innocent.

25

SNARKY NEW CATCHPHRASE, ANYONE?

TODAY WAS SCARY FINAL DAY FOR ME.

Biology.

If I didn't pass biology, it wouldn't matter if my YENT tryout ride was flawless. I *had* to get good grades. I turned away from the classroom door and leaned against the wall, squeezing my eyes shut and taking a deep breath.

"You okay?"

When I opened my eyes, Callie and Jacob were standing in front of me.

"Oh, yeah," I said. "Just getting ready to take my bio final."

Callie stepped closer to me, shifting her books from one arm to the other. "You're going to do *great*. I know it. Don't be nervous."

"You'll ace it," Jacob said. "You studied a ton."

"Right," I said. "True. Feeling less hyperventilate-y now. Thanks!"

They laughed as I walked into the classroom, feeling better. I sat down and took out a pen and paper. Jasmine walked by me, letting her big fat Coach bag bump against my shoulder.

"Oops," she said. "Sorry."

Right.

I ignored her and watched Julia and Alison take their seats in front of me. Neither girl turned around. My phone buzzed in my bag. Oops—that needed to be on silent. I leaned down to check my text.

U will rock it. G luck!

Eric. I turned down my phone and put it away.

"Getting last minute help?" Jasmine asked, turning to me.

"What?" I asked.

"Puh-lease. Who's texting you definitions for the test?"

I glared at her. "Excuse me? I can look at my phone whenever I want. And FYI, the texts have nothing to do with bio."

"Sure, Sasha. Not that you'd ever even be *able* to pull off a Julia-and-Alison."

Julia and Alison turned around and stared at Jas. "A *what*?" Julia snapped.

"You know what you did," Jasmine said. "We all know."

Julia's face reddened. "You don't know anything! And if you ever say that again, I'll—"

Julia closed her mouth when Ms. Peterson walked into the room. She eyed the four of us and Julia and Alison turned back around in their seats.

Ms. Peterson handed everyone in the front row a stack of test booklets to pass back. I pushed up my sleeves, ignoring my slamming heartbeat.

"Please open your test booklets and begin," Ms. Peterson said.

I flipped the page and stared at the first question. *What does DNA stand for?* Four choices. A, B, C, D. I filled in the bubble next to B, Deoxyribonucleic Acid, and went to the next question. I moved quickly through the multiple choice questions, determined to at least guess for a shot at credit if I didn't know the answer. Forty minutes later, Ms. Peterson cleared her throat.

"Pens and pencils down," she said. "Please make sure your name is on your booklet and pass them forward."

I handed my test to Julia and ran through answers in my head, trying to think if I'd missed anything. But there was nothing I could do now. The test was over. After all of the papers were turned in, I gathered my stuff and left. On my way out, I texted Eric.

Done! B @ stbl in 25 mins.

Already here, he texted back.

When I got to the stable, I hurried down the aisle and found Eric grooming Luna. He smiled when he saw me.

"How'd it go?" he asked.

"Not bad," I said. "I know I missed a few questions about cells, but I can't think of any sections I totally bombed."

"That's great." Eric said. "But now I'm *really* going to test you."

"Oh, you are?"

"Yep. I'm going to coach you on show jumping and *you* can work with me on cross-country."

I nodded. "Deal. But FYI, all of your finals are going to be easier than the course I'm going to make you jump."

Eric held back a laugh. "Go get Charm—I'll be ready in ten."

"You're on."

Exactly ten minutes later we were on horseback and heading to the outdoor arena. Mr. Conner had set up a new course with a couple of difficult combinations and I was ready to try it. Eric and I warmed up the horses and looked over the course.

"You can go first," I said.

Eric nodded. "Works for me." He took a breath and let Luna into a trot. A few strides later, she broke into a canter. Eric circled Luna before lining her up with the first three-foot vertical. Luna jumped easily over the red and white poles and Eric sat quietly in the saddle. Four strides later, Luna left the ground and hopped another vertical. Eric wobbled on the landing and his hands slid up her neck.

"C'mon," I whispered.

But Eric didn't recover in time. Luna reached the first half of a combination and took off a second too late. She tucked her forelegs under her body and her back hooves barely missed the top rail. Eric didn't have time to correct her before the second half of the combo. Luna was late again as she went into the air and she didn't tuck her forelegs enough. Her knees knocked the rail and it tumbled to the ground.

Eric collected Luna and got her over three more verticals and the final jump—an oxer—without another problem. Eric patted Luna's neck as he rode her over—the disappointment showed on his face.

"It's okay," I said. "Her timing was off, but that happens."

Eric halted Luna, nodding. But I noticed that he didn't say anything.

"Don't even worry about it," I said.

Eric smiled half-heartedly. "Your turn."

I settled into the saddle and let Charm into a canter. His even strides got us to the first vertical in seconds and Charm floated over the jump, landing softly on the other side. I pointed him at the next vertical, which was a few inches higher, and let him speed up enough to make it over. Charm, invigorated by the jump, tossed his head and sent his mane flying. Learning from Eric's mistake, I did a half halt and Charm flicked an ear back at me.

Three, two, one, and now! I got into the two-point position and Charm leaped into the air, the black rails flashing beneath us. My eyes were already on the second half of the obstacle before we even landed. When Charm hit the ground, I sank my weight into my heels and tried to keep Charm from rushing to the next jump. Two strides later, he rocked back on his haunches and propelled over the second half of the combo. He didn't come close to nicking the rail.

Charm eased into the turn and I gave him rein to let

him increase his speed a notch before the next vertical. But Charm's ears went forward and he slowed, tossing his mane playfully. I squeezed the reins and tightened my legs against his sides. Charm took four strides at a lazy pace before listening to me and focusing. He cleared the next three verticals and soared over the spread on the oxer without a problem.

I rode him back to Eric, shaking my head. "He stopped paying attention," I said. "Usually, I have to hold him back when we're on a course."

Eric looked at Charm, thinking. "Do you think he got bored in between jumps? Maybe work on keeping his attention, especially on longer turns and stretches with no jumps so that he doesn't lose interest and then scramble when he realizes there are more jumps."

"You're totally right," I said. "Good idea."

We let the horses walk out of the arena and I turned in the saddle to look at Eric. "I feel bad even asking you this, but would it be cool if we went to work at the creek instead of doing the cross-country course?"

"Why would you feel bad about that?" Eric asked. "It's a few days before the YENT—of course you want to practice as much as you can. We can do cross-country anytime. Let's go."

"Thanks." I said.

We walked the horses side by side down the dirt path through the woods. I let Charm wander on a loose rein and kicked my feet out of the stirrups, enjoying the quiet of the woods.

"This weekend's going to be crazy," I said.

Eric nodded. "Packing to go home *and* attempting to keep my parents from doing anything embarrassing while they're here."

"Ugh, don't say 'packing.' Paige and I have been doing that all week. Her stuff is in neat containers and mine is shoved into boxes and spilling everywhere."

Eric laughed. "So Sasha."

"When are your parents coming?" I guided Charm away from a patch of grass he was eyeing as he walked by.

"Sunday morning. I'll show them around campus— we didn't have much time to tour when I transferred, so they'll like that."

I considered asking Eric if he wanted to meet my parents. But I decided I'd wait for Paige's opinion before I pulled the trigger on that one.

We walked the horses closer to the creek. "Okay, I'm going to try to get Charm to go through the water," I said. "Will you pony us over if I can't get him to go?"

"Sure," Eric said.

I circled Charm away from the creek, then urged him into a trot. Charm trotted to the bank, slowed at the incline, and started to weave. I squeezed with both legs and tapped him with my heels. Hesitating, he started to lean back to slide to a stop. I deepened my seat and tried to push him forward. Charm shuddered, then bounded into the creek. Water splashed up his legs and I gripped with my knees to stay in the saddle. Charm plowed through the water, eager to get through it.

In two strides, Charm was out of the creek and scrambling up the bank. "Good boy!" I said, patting his neck.

"That was great!" Eric cheered.

Eric urged Luna through the creek and she barely made a splash.

"Show-off," I said, sticking out my tongue.

Eric reached over to squeeze my hand as we walked Charm and Luna through the woods.

After our ride we groomed and cooled the horses. Eric left for Blackwell and I walked back to Winchester. I went through the courtyard, lost in my own thoughts about the YENT, Eric, and what the summer would bring.

"Sasha?"

Jacob walked toward me, carrying a giant plastic cup of soda and a bag of Doritos.

"Marathon studying session food?"

Jacob nodded. "Absolutely. I want to go to a video-game tournament this summer in Boston and there's no way my parents will let me go if I don't get good grades."

"I'm sure you will," I said. "Are they picking you up Sunday?"

"Yeah. When do your parents get here?"

"Tomorrow afternoon. I was thinking about . . ."

Oh, no. Did *not* want to talk to Jacob about this.

"About what?"

But it was too late and I was the *worst* liar.

"Oh, uh, just maybe inviting Eric to lunch with them. With my, um, parents. I haven't decided."

Jacob shook his head. "Wow. It must be superserious if you're taking *that* step."

"It isn't that big of a deal," I said. Was it? And even if it was, why was I trying to convince Jacob about *anything*?

"You haven't been going out that long," he said.

"Oh. Yeah . . . I guess." How long *was* I supposed to wait?

Jacob shrugged and took a drink. "It just seems fast.

Like it might freak out a guy to meet his girlfriend's parents so soon. But do whatever you want, obviously. Whatever. I've got to go."

I nodded, dazed. "Okay. Bye."

I hadn't even thought about how it would make Eric feel to meet my parents. We really *hadn't* been dating that long—maybe it would make him nervous.

26

LOOK WHO CAME
TO LUNCH

"WE'RE SO DONE!" I CHEERED. IT WAS JUST
after ten on Friday morning. Seventh grade was officially
over.

"I know!" Paige said. We practically skipped out of the
history building. "See ya, seventh grade!"

"Finals are done. No more tests. Or essays. Or homework. Or projects. Or anything school-related, all summer. Omigod." I shifted the pile of books and papers in
my arms.

Paige shook her head as we walked down the cobble-
stone path and under the archway and started toward
Winchester. "I can't even believe it. I'm in shock. We're
going to be *eighth* graders next year!"

"That sounds so much older," I said. I took a deep

breath and looked up the sky, enjoying the gold warmth of the sun on my face.

"Totally."

We laughed, but my smile slipped when I saw Jasmine and the Belles walking in our direction. The girls stopped and looked at Paige and me.

"Sasha," Violet said, fake smiling. "Ready for summer?"

I nodded, not having anything to say to Violet. When I kept walking away, Violet held up her hand. Brianna, Georgia, and Jasmine blocked the sidewalk behind her.

Violet ran a French-manicured hand through her light brown hair. "So, what are you doing this summer?"

"Riding at YENT camp," I answered.

The Belles and Jasmine burst into laughter. Paige and I glared at them.

"Or," Jasmine said. "You could tell the truth. You know, how you're going back to Union where you'll ride Charm in circles in a tiny pen for three months."

Georgia smirked. "Why so glum? Isn't that what you're accustomed to?"

I stepped off the sidewalk and into the grass, staring straight ahead as Paige walked alongside me. I could have made a comment how none of the Belles had even been asked to try out for the YENT, but it wasn't worth it.

"Don't listen to them," Paige said. "We know you're going to make it."

"I don't care what they think," I said. "I'm *not* going back to Union."

"Good. Because you don't have time to worry about them. You've got to get ready for your parents."

Inside our room I stepped around boxes, plastic trunks, and suitcases. I was mostly packed except for the clothes I needed for today and tomorrow.

We changed into jeans and T-shirts and started emptying everything but the essentials from our bathroom drawers and closets. I grabbed my stack of DVDs off the TV stand and walked over to Paige.

"Here," I said, holding them out. "You can give them back this fall."

Paige's eyes landed on the DVDs. "Sasha, no way. I can't take those. My mom won't let me watch anything that's not on PBS, you know that."

Ignoring Paige, I opened her suitcase and started layering the DVDs between her clothes. "You're taking them. And watch them in your room on your laptop or something. You need *City Girls*, Paige. Don't argue."

Paige clutched one of the DVDs to her chest. "Okay,

okay. I would have died if I hadn't been able to watch that episode where Josh *finally* kissed Ara."

My phone buzzed.

Dad and I are waiting in the parking lot!

I put my phone back in my pocket. "They're here. My last moments of freedom." I sighed dramatically and Paige giggled.

"Oh, go already," she teased, waving me out the door.

"Sasha!" Mom called from the parking lot. She waved and clutched Dad's arm. Dad, beside her, held up his camera and started snapping photos.

"Dad! You promised—"

He put his camera down so I could hug him with one arm and Mom with the other.

"We missed you, honey," Mom said. She ran her hand over my hair.

"I missed you guys too," I said. "But soon, you'll be stuck with me. For just a little while, hopefully."

"We'll take as much time as we can get," Dad said. A gurgle came from his stomach and he put a hand over it.

"Oops," he said. "I skipped my usual pancake breakfast this morning."

"Daaad." I hugged him. "Let's go get lunch."

"We're ready," Mom said.

We walked the long way to the dining hall, which was run like a restaurant during special occasions. Since parents were in town, Canterwood had hostesses and waiters on staff for the weekend to make the atmosphere even more impressive. I kept an eye out for Eric—even though he was supposed to be back at his dorm—remembering Jacob's advice.

The hostess seated us and, after Dad spent fifteen minutes convincing Mom that having a salad with his steak *did* make it a healthy meal, we ordered our food. The hall felt like a five-star restaurant. Sunshine spilled through the windows and made the hardwood floor gleam. Fresh orchids were in crystal vases on every table and there wasn't an empty seat in the room.

"This is wonderful," Mom said, taking a bite of her white grilled cheese sandwich. We'd both ordered the same thing.

"Totally," I said. "So, are you guys ready for me to come home?"

Mom and Dad smiled at each other. "Your mom has been making sure the kitchen is stuffed with all of your favorite foods and she . . ."

But Dad's voice started to sound fuzzy when I glanced across the room and saw Callie, her parents, and *Jacob* walk into the dining room. Jacob stood next to Callie's dad and laughed at something he said.

The hostess led them to their table and Jacob pulled out a chair for Callie. He sat next to Callie, who looked very girly and pretty in a simple black spaghetti-strap dress accessorized with a skinny silver belt.

I couldn't stop watching. They were all so comfortable with each other. Jacob didn't seem at *all* freaked out to be dining with Callie's parents. I couldn't figure him out—it was like I didn't even know him anymore. But I didn't care that he was eating with Callie's parents, right?

"Sasha?" Mom touched my arm. "You okay?"

I tore my eyes away from Jacob and the Harpers. "Yeah, sorry. I just saw some friends. What were you saying?"

"Do you want to go talk to them?" Dad asked.

"No!" I said.

Oops. That was a little loud.

"I mean, I can talk to them later," I said. "What were you saying?"

Mom stared at me for a second, as if her sometimes-annoying-yet-always-accurate Mom radar knew something was off. "Dad and I are glad to be here and we want to see you," she said. "But we also know that you have a big day tomorrow and you probably want to practice instead of hanging out with your parents."

"I don't want to leave you guys, but yeah—I'll probably start to feel anxious if I don't ride soon."

"We'll go back to the hotel to unwind and get ready for tomorrow," Dad said. "We'll talk to you tonight—we want to wish you luck before you go to sleep."

On our way out of the dining room, I saw Jacob's eyes flicker across the room at me. Instead of looking away, I held his gaze—staring at him until I passed the table.

Why would Jacob have made me feel so insecure about Eric meeting my parents when he seemed so comfortable with Callie's?

27

SASHA SILVER,
SHRINK

BY THE TIME CHARM AND I ARRIVED BEHIND
the stable, Callie and Heather were already working Jack
and Aristocrat at opposite ends of the arena.

"Where's Jas?" I asked, going for the obvious question.

"She went out on the cross-country course with the
Belles," Heather said.

"Fine by me," Callie said. "At least she's not in the
arena with us."

We walked our horses and I sneaked a glance at Callie and
Heather. Callie looked calm, as always, and not a hint of ner-
vousness about tomorrow showed on her face. But Heather
looked a little pale and she kept fidgeting in the saddle.

"No matter what happens tomorrow," I said. "We did
everything we could."

Heather rolled her eyes. "You sound like a shrink. More riding, less talking."

"Do you guys want to critique each other?" Callie asked.

Heather and I nodded enthusiastically. Clearly some nervous energy to burn.

"We're ready," I said. "Let's take turns picking exercises."

Once I finished warming Charm up, Heather walked Aristocrat next to him and her horse laid back his ears. "Figure eights," she said. "I want to start with those."

We distanced the horses and worked them through the pattern. First at a walk, then a trot and, finally, large figure eights at a canter.

Heather slowed Aristocrat and watched Callie. "Watch your leg position. They keep sliding forward when you turn."

Callie nodded and did the pattern again. I wanted to work on transitions next, so we called out to each other when to slow the horses or change gaits. We rode for another forty-five minutes before stopping.

"I'm going for water," Heather said. "Later."

Heather walked Aristocrat out of the arena and Callie stopped Jack beside me. "Heather was riding when I got here," she said. "Aristocrat was sweaty and it looked as if they'd been here awhile already."

"She wants this so bad," I said. "But still, she shouldn't overpractice."

"I know." Callie rubbed Jack's neck. "But it's hard to stop when we're *this* close."

We were quiet for a minute, letting the horses rest. Callie looked as though she was about to say something, then sighed and picked at a nonexistent tangle in Jack's mane.

"Is something wrong?" I asked.

Callie twirled her fingers in Jack's mane. "I don't know. Maybe. Jacob has been acting kind of weird for the past few days."

"Weird, how?"

"He just seems worried about something. Or nervous, I don't know. Whenever I ask him if anything's wrong, he always says no."

"I'm sure he's just stressed about finals and getting ready to go home for the summer. Everyone's under a lot of pressure right now," I said. But even as I said it, I wasn't sure I believed it. Jacob had been acting strange for a while. I'd thought it was just weirdness with Eric, but now I wasn't so sure.

Callie nodded. "I'm sure you're right. And he *is* taking me out for a good luck dinner tonight."

"See, that'll be fun! Is he coming to watch you ride?"

"He is," Callie said. "I even told him where the good seats are."

I was glad to see Callie looking less worried. She definitely didn't need any more major stress before tomorrow.

"Are you up for cooling them out and braiding their manes and tails?" Callie asked. "It'll take too long in the morning."

"Yeah," I said. "They haven't been to see their stylists in a while."

Giggling, we dismounted.

"I think we should glitter their manes and add some highlights," Callie said. "Thoughts?"

"Charm's always wanted to go blond," I said. "And the scouts will love it."

After braiding manes and tails with Callie, I spent an hour cleaning Charm's tack. I polished his saddle and bridle until they were supple and gleaming. When I got back to Winchester, Paige, aka the best roommate ever, distracted me with *Tokyo Girl* reruns and manicures. Paige painted my nails in OPI's Princesses Rule and I did hers in Bubble Bath.

"Look at your sparkly nails if you get nervous," Paige said. "And remember the name of the polish. You're going to rock it tomorrow."

I smiled at her. "Thanks, P."

Paige, inspecting her nails, got up and went to the door. "I'm going to grab us chips and salsa. Then, start a movie?"

"Awesome. But don't mess up your nails!"

Paige left and I flopped backward onto my bed. Paige had been working overtime all day to distract me from thinking about testing.

My phone buzzed and I opened it.

Don't even worry abt 2mrw. You've got this. C u in the mrning!

I texted Eric back.

:)

I kept rereading his text until Paige came back.

You've got this.

I've got this.

28

LUCKY CHARMS

IT WAS STILL DARK OUTSIDE WHEN I WALKED into the stable. Horses blinked sleepily at me as I passed them on my way to check on Charm. I peered over the stall door to look at him and he was asleep, facing the back of his stall. He could sleep for a few more minutes while I walked the show jumping course.

I left the stable and crossed the yard to the outdoor arena. The sun was just peeking over the campus and I wrapped my sweatshirt-covered arms across my chest. It was still chilly in the early morning. Taking a deep breath, I started walking and counting strides between jumps. *Four strides between the vertical and the double oxer,* I thought.

I paused, looking at the entrance to the arena. I flashed back to my first day at Canterwood and how Charm had gotten loose and galloped past this arena. He'd spooked Aristocrat and Heather had fallen. What an awful start that had been! And now, I was about to try out for the YENT. That day last September seemed like years ago. I'd been the scared new girl, terrified to make even one mistake and be sent home. Now I knew I belonged at Canterwood.

I walked the rest of the course and went back to the stable for Charm's tack box. I set the box in the aisle by a free pair of crossties and went to get Charm.

"Today's it, boy," I said, unlatching his stall door and sliding it open. "You okay?"

Charm lowered his head so I could hug his neck. I led him into the aisle and clipped the crossties to his halter. I was picking stray pieces of hay out of his braids when Callie walked down the aisle with Jack.

"Hey," she said. "Ready?"

I nodded. "Hope so. Are you nervous?"

Callie crosstied Jack and turned to me. "Um, yeah! But grooming Jack always makes me feel better."

I tried to take a deep breath. Fail.

"Hey, YENT girls," someone called.

I looked up and saw Eric smiling at us. He patted Jack's neck, then walked over to Charm and me.

"Hi," Callie and I said.

"How's it going?" Eric asked.

"Good so far," I said. "I've got to groom Charm, tack him up, and then change."

"I'll groom him for you if you need to do something else," Eric said.

"Thanks. But grooming him is part of the ritual. If I didn't, I'd feel like I'd missed a step. Bonding time."

Eric nodded. "I understand. Anything else I can do?"

I gave him my sweetest smile. "Get dessert with me tonight after it's all over?"

"Done," Eric said.

Eric wished us luck one more time and headed off to help Mr. Conner.

I reached into my tack box and pulled out my Absorbine Supershine hoof polish to paint Charm's hooves. When I finished, I stepped back and looked him over. Every hair on his chestnut coat gleamed like copper. His blaze was bright white and his shiny black hooves popped.

"After I tack him up, can you hold Charm while I change?" I asked Callie.

"Sure thing," she said. "I'll go after you."

I went to the tack room and came back with Charm's saddle, bridle, and white saddle pad. I smoothed the pad onto his back and lifted the English saddle onto it. Charm didn't move as I tightened the girth. He lowered his head while I unclipped the crossties and slipped the reins over his head. He was being extra sweet—probably because he knew it was an important day. I finished bridling Charm and led him over to Callie.

"Be right back," I said. I grabbed my clothes from the hanging rack in the tack room and changed in the bathroom. I'd picked my new fawn-colored breeches, high black boots, new white dress shirt, and navy blue show jacket. I pulled my hair into a low bun and applied clear gloss.

I emerged from the bathroom and Callie had Jack tacked up. I held both horses while she put on her show clothes. When Callie came back, she was staring at her phone screen and frowning.

"What's wrong?" I asked.

"I just thought Jacob would be here by now," Callie said. "And . . ."

"And?" I prompted. "You can tell me."

Callie's eyes filled with tears. "He canceled our date last night without any reason. He'd been so excited about taking me out, then he texted me at the last minute and said he couldn't make it."

"Oh, Callie. I'm so sorry." I reached over to touch her arm. "Why didn't you tell me before?"

"Because it's a big day. I didn't want to bring it up before we started riding."

I shook my head. "Puh-leeze. You're my BFF—this is what we do! Did you ask him why?"

"He just said he had last minute 'things' to do before he went home. He said he was sorry, but he just couldn't make it."

"I'm so sorry. I know finals are over, but maybe there's something up with his parents or his roommate. *Whatever* it is, you can't stress about it right now."

Callie wiped her eyes and nodded. "Right. I can talk to Jacob after the tryouts."

"You totally can. Plus, you'll be so much less stressed."

"Thanks, Sash."

"Anytime."

Callie and I led Jack and Charm down the aisle and toward the big window that overlooked the outdoor arena. Callie's parents were in the front row, whispering to each other. They looked more nervous than Callie.

In the next row, a tall man sat next to a woman who had Jasmine's wavy dark hair, but wore a shirt patterned with giant purple and pink flowers paired with white capris. Yikes—Jas's sense of fashion definitely didn't come naturally. Mom and Dad sat by Callie's parents.

"This is really happening," Callie whispered. "This is our shot at the YENT."

"Don't remind me!" I said, bumping my shoulder against Callie's. "Are you *trying* to freak me out?"

Callie laughed. "Sorry, sorry. But we'll be out there in a few minutes! Did we forget anything?"

"Um," I looked at our clothes. Then I glanced at the horses. "Bridles, saddles, saddle pads, hoof polish . . . oh! Fly spray." I handed Charm's reins to Callie. "I'll go get it."

I jogged down the aisle and stopped when muffled voices came through the door.

"Heather, I did *not* skip my meeting in Los Angeles to watch you fail."

I cringed. Mr. Fox.

"You will not embarrass me. Mr. Nicholson will be calling your name as part of that team tomorrow," Mr. Fox continued, his voice low. "I mean it, Heather. If you don't, I—"

I couldn't take another second! I pushed open the door, hurrying into the room. Heather was almost up against the wall, Mr. Fox towering over her. Her face was as white as Charm's new saddle pad. Mr. Fox glared at me, but I ignored him and walked over to Heather.

"Oh, my God, what's your problem?" I asked Heather,

folding my arms. She turned to look at me, her eyes asking me not to leave.

"What?" she whispered, her voice wavering a little.

"How could you blow me off last night?" I made sure not to look at Mr. Fox. "That's the third time this week! You keep saying you'll come to the movies with me, but you never do. Are you, like, obsessed with practicing or something?"

Heather's eyes locked on mine. Relief flashed across her face for a brief second before turning to fake annoyance.

"Calm down, Sasha. I had more important things to do than see a stupid movie. The YENT is all I've been thinking about for months."

"But you're *always* here." I pretend-pouted.

"Maybe that's because I came to Canterwood to ride, not goof off and have fun."

Mr. Fox's gaze shifted between us. He stepped forward and looked as if he was about to say something when his BlackBerry rang.

"Fox," he said into the phone. He stomped away from us and slammed the tack room door behind him.

I walked around Heather and nabbed the fly spray from the top shelf. I wanted to say something, but didn't want to embarrass her. I knew she had to be upset that I'd seen any of that. I started to the door.

"Sasha," Heather said.

I turned and saw something different in her expression—almost as if she was seeing me as a friend for once.

"Don't even—" I started.

"Thanks," she mouthed.

I shut the door behind me and went back to Callie. I sprayed Charm with fly spray and did the same to Jack, not saying a word about what I'd seen.

"Look at all the people out there now," Callie said, pointing to the stands.

Jacob sat alone at the end of the stands, near Mr. Fox who stood and paced with the phone pressed against his ear. At the bottom of the stands, Paige and Eric were sitting together—far away from Mom and Dad. I'd told Paige about how I'd wanted to keep them apart, just for now, and she'd promised to do her best.

Julia and Alison were there too.

"I can't even imagine how they must feel watching this," I said.

"Me neither," Callie said. "They must be thinking about how different things would have been today if it hadn't been for that test."

Hoofbeats clattered down the aisle and stopped behind

us. I turned and Jasmine stood there, shaking her head. Phoenix stood quietly beside her.

"What?" I asked.

"It's just amusing to me that you and Callie even still bother."

Callie and I didn't respond. Heather appeared with Aristocrat, and soon, Mr. Conner and Mr. Nicholson, the head YENT scout, walked up to us. Mr. Nicholson looked like an older version of Mr. Conner—tan, but with a shock of silver hair.

"Good morning, girls," Mr. Nicholson said. "I want to wish you all luck with your test. Try not to be too nervous. Just pretend it's any other lesson."

Heather, Callie, Jasmine, and I nodded, knowing we'd never be able to do that.

Mr. Nicholson nodded to us, turned, and walked out of the stable.

"Ready?" Mr. Conner asked.

All any of us could do was nod.

"We'll start with dressage, then show jumping. After that, we'll take a break before moving out to the cross-country course."

I was glad to get dressage—my weakest area—over first.

"I'm proud of each of you," Mr. Conner said. "I hope you realize how talented you are to even get to this point. Whether you make it or not, you are all dedicated riders. That's more important to me than whether or not you make this team."

Mr. Conner motioned for us to follow him outside to the arena. I let Callie, Heather, and Jasmine walk in front of me, needing one more minute with Charm. "We can do this, right, boy?" I asked Charm.

Charm blinked at me with a calming gaze. I looked at my wrist and rubbed the bracelet charms—I needed as much luck as I could get.

29

THE SPARKLE FACTOR

MR. CONNER WALKED INTO THE CENTER OF the arena and motioned for Heather, Jasmine, Callie, and me to walk our horses out to the rail.

This.

Was.

It.

I kept my eyes forward and didn't look at anyone.

"Please take a few minutes to warm up your horses," Mr. Conner said. "And I'll explain to the audience about today's testing."

I angled Charm behind Aristocrat and we began our warm-up.

"Welcome, everyone," Mr. Conner said. "I'm pleased that you chose to join us. First, the students will be working through dressage. Mr. Nicholson will be looking for several factors in each ride. He'll be watching for ease and freedom of movement, lightness of the horse's forehand, and a deep level of engagement between horse and rider."

Callie was riding first, so Heather, Jasmine, and I trotted our horses out of the arena. I stopped Charm a few yards away—close, but not too close.

Mr. Conner didn't need to call out the test to Callie—she knew every movement. Jack looked great and it was a near perfect ride until they made their first circle. It was a meter too big. Then, minutes later, Jack's next circle looked a half meter too small. That wasn't possible—maybe the circles just looked off from here?

Callie finished her test and rode out of the arena to applause. But I only needed to look at her face for a second to know that she was upset with her ride. I wanted to talk to her now, but I knew she needed a few minutes alone. Heather, Jasmine, and I approached the entrance—waiting to find out who was riding next.

"Sasha," Mr. Conner said. "You're up."

I entered the arena and rode to the X. I stopped and saluted. I couldn't give up one second of focus. When I'd imagined this moment, I thought I'd be freaking out. But instead, I was calm. I'd done everything I could to prepare. Now, it was up to Charm and me to prove it.

"Working trot to C," Mr. Conner called. "Track right and ten-meter circle at B."

Charm trotted forward with even steps. We made our circle and Mr. Conner directed us to do a collected canter. That wasn't easy for Charm—or me. But I asked him to raise his neck and he arched it. Charm felt light under my hands and his stride was as short as it needed to be.

Mr. Conner asked us for a free walk, working canter on the left lead, and a twenty-meter circle. Charm's canter was heavier than I wanted, but I shook it off and focused on the rest of the exercises. I concentrated on the turns since Charm often tried to drift. I only had to correct him through one turn. This felt like it was one of our best tests ever!

"Medium walk to X and halt," Mr. Conner said. I stopped Charm in the center of the arena and saluted again. Charm, knowing he had to stand still, didn't even blink until I relaxed the reins and let him walk out of the arena. Cheering erupted from the stands and I looked over my shoulder at my parents, Eric, and Paige. They were standing and clapping.

I stopped Charm a few yards out of the arena and dismounted. I hugged him, not caring that he'd cover my show coat with hair. I looked over and saw Callie walking Jack in slow circles. Still, I knew Callie around shows—she'd talk to me when she was ready.

"You were so great," I told Charm. "I love you, boy."

Charm blew a gentle breath into my hand. "Phase one is over. Now, we get to do all of the fun stuff. *Our* stuff," I told him. "Cross-country." Charm's ears went forward.

"*That* was dressage?" Jasmine asked, riding by. "Wow." She laughed and trotted Phoenix into the arena when Mr. Conner called her name. I just rolled my eyes and walked Charm closer to the arena. Now that my test was over, I could enjoy watching Jasmine and Heather ride.

Even though Jas had lost her rough style, her movements were too sharp. Phoenix didn't seem to be in synch with her—he moved because he was afraid of her. Five minutes into the test, the gelding started sweating and his chest turned a steely gray. But Jas, always a pro, finished without any major mistakes and she exited the arena with a smile.

Heather's dressage test was one of the best I'd ever seen her complete. Her signals were invisible. Aristocrat moved through the test as if *he'd* memorized it, but was still spontaneous and he flowed through every turn and circle. I looked up at the stands to watch Mr. Fox. He leaned forward in his seat, studying Heather's test. The way he watched her made me squirm. He wasn't appreciating her ride—he was judging her every move.

Heather finished her test and saluted. People started clapping and Heather looked into the stands. Everyone—especially Julia and Alison—was applauding.

Except for Mr. Fox.

In the seconds since Heather had finished her test, he'd managed to make a phone call. He had a hand over one ear and his phone against the other. Julia and Alison, glancing over and seeing Mr. Fox, started cheering louder and waving, trying to distract Heather from looking at her dad. But Heather had already seen Mr. Fox.

Worst dad ever much? And I didn't even want to think about how Heather must have felt not to have her mom here. Callie had said she'd overheard Julia and Alison talking about how Mrs. Fox had decided to attend a country club party instead of Heather's testing. Niiice.

Heather straightened in the saddle and walked Aristocrat out of the exit.

"Great ride," I said when she passed me.

"Thanks." Heather half smiled. "You weren't horrible either."

Mr. Conner stepped into the center of the arena and

turned to the stands. "That concludes our dressage round. If you'll follow me over to the larger arena, we'll begin jumping in a few minutes."

Jasmine and Heather trotted their horses forward and I let Charm hang back so we could walk over with Callie and Jack.

"I know you're upset," I said. "But every other part of your test was perfect."

Callie shook her head. "That doesn't matter. The circles were so off—Mr. Nicholson probably isn't even considering me after that."

"Yes, he is. We still have two rounds left," I said. "Plus, Mr. Nicholson has seen you ride dressage before and he knows you can have an almost perfect round."

Callie nodded. "That's true." She looked toward the stands. "And Jacob's here."

I nodded. "He was definitely watching."

We let the horses walk on a loose rein to the arena and we waited for our parents, friends, and Mr. Nicholson to get seated. My eyes settled on Mr. Nicholson's leather-bound folder. He'd been writing notes during all of our tests. What had he written about me? I didn't have long to wonder, because Mr. Conner walked up to us.

"Your jumping order has been determined," he said.

"Heather, you'll go first. Then, Jasmine, Callie, and Sasha. Heather, you may start whenever you're ready."

Heather trotted Aristocrat into the arena and let him into a canter. She pointed him at the first vertical and Aristocrat took it with ease and cantered toward the second jump. Heather and Aristocrat cleared jump after jump, not even coming close to knocking a rail.

I shook my head in amazement. I'd worried that Mr. Fox's behavior would have rattled Heather. But it looked like it had actually fueled her drive to do better. Aristocrat and Heather's futures were on the line, and the way Heather was jumping, she wasn't putting either of them at risk.

Heather finished her ride and the cheering started the second Aristocrat's hooves hit the ground. Heather rubbed Aristocrat's neck and trotted him out of the arena. She slowed him to a walk as she passed us.

"That was amazing," Callie said to Heather. "Mr. Nicholson was impressed—I could see it on his face."

Heather started to smile at Callie, but caught herself. "Duh, Harper." She dismounted and led Aristocrat a few yards away.

I watched Jasmine and Phoenix enter the arena. Callie and I were silent as Jasmine and Phoenix started. Jasmine didn't make one mistake. She encouraged Phoenix when he needed it, urged him when he started to slow on long turns, and never wobbled on landings. She even finished the course a few seconds faster than Heather, though timing wasn't a factor today.

"That's going to be tough to beat," Callie said. She adjusted the reins and prepared to ride Jack into the arena.

"You can do it," I said. "You've totally got this."

Mr. Conner nodded to her and she sat still for a second before urging Jack into a trot. She let him into a canter and pointed him at the first jump. I crossed my fingers that she would make Jasmine's ride look awful. Over the twelve jumps, Jack did everything Callie asked. He didn't knock a rail or come close to touching the faux brush with his hooves.

But something—not anything technical, but *something*— was off. Jasmine's and Heather's rides had been fiery. But Callie's ride had lacked the usual Callie sparkle. It could have been anyone else's ride. And that wasn't like Callie.

When she finished, she rode over to me and rubbed Jack's neck. "Not one rail down!" she cheered.

"You were amazing," I said. "I'm so proud of you."

Callie dismounted and looked toward the stands.

"You're going to do great. I'm taking Jack over by Jacob and I'll watch from there."

Before I could respond, Callie led Jack in Jacob's direction. Jacob climbed down from the stands and hugged Callie. After watching them for a few seconds, I looked away and went back to concentrating on my own ride.

Mr. Conner motioned to me to come to the arena entrance. I trotted Charm up to Mr. Conner and he patted Charm's neck.

"Have a good ride," he said. "Don't rush the jumps and stay relaxed. You're going to do great."

I tried to smile, but I was too nervous. Instead, I nodded and rode Charm into the arena. The course usually seemed endless before I got started, but by the second jump, I was always ready for more.

I tapped my heels against Charm's sides and gave him rein. He moved into a collected canter and headed for the first jump—a simple vertical. Charm jumped it and stayed calm as he took the next two verticals—both three feet high—and then cantered toward the first oxer. I let Charm's pace quicken a notch to give him speed to get over the spread. He sailed over the black and white rails of the oxer and landed almost without a sound on the other side.

We turned back, took a brush jump, and then tackled a vertical with yellow rails and flower boxes on the sides.

Charm flicked an ear back to me as I gathered him before the double combination. This was one of the trickiest combos. I started counting strides. *Five, four, three, two, one, and now!* I let Charm go and he bounced over the first jump, took two strides, and surged into the air for the second half. I listened for a rail to fall behind us, but the only sound was Charm's hooves pounding the dirt.

Charm, not even winded, leaped the oxer, second brush jump, and a vertical with blue and white rails without pause. *Three jumps left,* I thought. *We're almost there!* I didn't let myself think about the final jump—a triple combo.

I angled Charm in front of a plain red and white vertical and rose in the saddle. Charm jumped and landed, but gained too much speed before the next obstacle. I did a half halt and he responded by slowing and not rushing the last vertical. He huffed when we landed and swished his tail, knowing we were close to the end.

He cantered around the final turn. My brain was already on the combination. *Don't mess up the combo.* We were *thisclose* to a clean ride. Then, Charm's stride faltered. He pointed both ears away from me and his once forward, smooth canter became bouncy and uneven. I squeezed my legs against his sides and moved the reins in my fingers. Charm was getting bored on the last long turn. The first jump of the combination was strides away—there were seconds to get his focus.

I shifted in the saddle, forcing my weight down, and I tapped Charm with my heels. We turned toward the first jump and he started to regain momentum.

We've got it, I thought. *He'll make it through the triple.*

At just the right moment, Charm propelled himself over the first jump. But he landed too close. There wasn't enough room in between jumps to increase his speed. Charm tried to jump the second part of the combination, but his knees knocked into the rail. It tumbled to the ground.

I had no time to obsess—the next jump was right there. Charm, with a gallant effort, pushed off high into the air and fought to clear the last part of the triple combination. I was sure he'd take down the rail with his back hooves, but he managed to get over it. We landed on the other side and the rail stayed in place.

No one else had knocked a rail. I tried not to look as disappointed as I felt. Patting Charm's neck, I looked up into the stands at Eric.

Good job, Eric mouthed.

I managed a smile and nodded. *Remember what you just told Callie,* I reminded myself. Mr. Nicholson had seen Charm and me jump before. And I couldn't forget that cross-country was next. The only scary spot would be the creek, but I was ready.

Mr. Conner stepped in front of the stands. "Thank you all for watching our jumping round," he said. "We're going to take a break for a couple of hours to rest the horses and riders. Please feel free to grab lunch on campus and meet us back at the stable entrance at two."

As everyone started to descend from the portable stands, Mr. Conner walked over to us. "Wonderful job, girls," he said. "Your hard work was evident."

Everyone but Jasmine smiled. She looked as if someone told her she was an amazing rider *every* day and this was old news to her.

"Mike and Doug will cool and water your horses," Mr. Conner said. "You may get lunch with your parents if you like, but please be on time to start."

I hugged Charm, and as I handed his reins to Mike, Paige and Eric ran up to me.

"Omigod," Paige said, grabbing me in a hug. "You were sooo awesome! I have no idea how you get over all of those jumps without knocking them down. *And* you never got confused about what jump to take."

I hugged her back. "Just like how I don't get how you can make a lemon meringue pie without burning it or messing up the ingredients."

Eric squeezed my hand. "That was such a great ride. I never would have been able to get Charm over that triple combo after he stopped paying attention. Amazing, Sash."

"Thanks. I'm so proud of Charm."

I looked over his shoulder and saw Mom and Dad starting to make their way over.

Don't panic, don't panic! But I didn't want them to meet Eric yet. *Think of something!*

"Uh, Eric, Mr. Conner waved at you," I said.

"He did?" Eric asked, looking over at Mr. Conner, who had his back to us.

I nodded, feeling my face go pink. "He just turned and motioned for you. He must need your help or something."

"Okaaay. I guess I'll go talk to him. Catch you later," Eric said.

Phew.

Mom and Dad reached us just as Eric found Mr. Conner. I crossed my fingers that Mr. Conner would find something for Eric to do that would keep him busy for a while.

"That was a gorgeous ride, honey," Mom said. "You and Charm looked so good together." She handed me an old jacket to cover up my show coat. I had a habit of spilling lunch on my clothes during show day.

Dad held up his Nikon. "I took lots of photos. Gram and Grandpa are going to love them."

This was kind of a big day, so I'd let him slide on taking lots of pics. Just this once.

"Do you want to get lunch with us, or wait here?" Mom asked. "If I know my daughter, I bet she wants to stay close to Charm and let us bring her back something to eat."

I laughed. "You might know me just a little, Mom. Burger and chocolate milkshake?"

"You got it," Mom said. She knew I needed my energy food before cross-country.

"Can we get you the same, Paige?" Dad asked.

"Sure," Paige said. "Thanks."

Mom and Dad started for the cafeteria and I watched until they were far away from Eric.

"Let's go sit in the hayloft," I suggested. "I'll text them where we are."

Paige and I started across the yard to the stable. As we walked, I looked for Heather, Callie, and Jasmine. Jasmine and her parents had vanished—probably going off campus for a fancy lunch or something. By the arena, Mr. Fox was talking to Mr. Conner. Heather stared at her boots, not even glancing up at Mr. Conner.

Paige saw it too. "But look who's coming," she said.

Julia and Alison hurried over to Heather—they knew she needed a rescue. Heather walked away with them, leaving Mr. Conner to handle Mr. Fox.

30

WHO'S THE LIAR?

THE TWO-HOUR BREAK BLEW BY AND AFTER Paige and I had stuffed ourselves with burgers and milkshakes, Eric found us to say good luck before my final round. I said good-bye to everyone and went to hang out with Charm. We needed a few minutes alone.

I stood with Charm in his stall, my arm draped over his neck. I'd taken him from Mike and had led him back in here. Charm kept shooting longing glances at his hay net.

"Sorry, boy," I said. "You can't eat right now. After today, you're going to have a few days off. And then, we'll either spend the summer working together at Briar Creek in Union or we'll go to YENT camp."

Just saying the words "YENT camp" made me smile.

"We better get out there."

I tightened Charm's girth, then bent down to check his leg wraps. On our way down the aisle, I grabbed my protective vest off the hook and buckled it on. Mom, Dad, Paige, Eric, and the rest of everyone's friends and family were all waiting at the finish line. Mr. Nicholson was out on the course by an undisclosed jump to watch.

Heather, Jasmine, Callie, and I mounted our horses and rode them up to Mr. Conner.

"Sasha, you're going first," Mr. Conner said. "You may begin in one moment. This is the last round. I want to see safe rides out there."

We all nodded. Charm was made for cross-country. Even though it was the end of a long day and he had to be tired, I knew he'd put everything into this round.

"Sasha, please head to the starting line," Mr. Conner instructed.

Charm danced sideways, tossing his head and almost prancing to the line. He was *so* ready. But was I? I'd walked the course twice and knew Charm could get over all of the jumps and make great time, but I worried about the creek. I shook out my hands. *Don't think about that now.* I'd deal with it when Charm and I were there.

I pushed down my heels, sank my weight into the saddle and gripped the reins—readying myself in case

Charm bolted. Mr. Conner raised his arm above his head, then dropped his hand. When his hand went down, I loosened the reins and Charm surged forward, almost throwing me back in the saddle. I held him at a medium canter, not wanting to let him burn out before we even got started.

Charm jumped easily over two brush fences and trotted uphill. When we hit level ground, he broke into a canter and jumped an old gate with blue paint peeling off the wooden planks. His strides were rhythmic as he cantered toward two hay bale jumps, the first lower than the second. I'd always half-expected Charm to try and snatch a mouthful of hay in midleap. But he tucked his knees neatly under his body and got over the hay bales.

I slowed him to a trot and leaned back in the saddle as we started down the hill. The grass changed to dirt and we trotted into the woods and along a winding path. Charm eased around a sharp corner and had two strides to straighten out before he jumped a log pile.

"Good boy," I said. I tried to keep the nerves out of my voice. The creek was one jump away. Charm tugged on the reins, asking for more, and I let him out a notch. He gathered himself and launched over a small fallen tree that Mr. Conner had left blocking part of the trail.

I urged him with my hands, encouraging his momentum so he'd keep going right through the creek.

We trotted down a slight incline and Charm approached the bank. The dirt softened and I stopped posting to sit to his trot while he moved forward. I drove him with my legs, but tried not to clamp onto his sides.

Charm's ears started flicking back and forth, but he didn't weave. The clear creek water flowed over the shiny pebble rock bed and the few sunrays that had broken through the trees bounced off the water.

A stride before the creek, Charm hesitated and started to sink his weight backward. "No, you've got it," I said. "C'mon!"

Charm seemed to trot in place for a second before bounding into the creek. Water sprayed into the air, soaking the lower half of my breeches and trickling into my boots, but I didn't care. Charm plunged through the knee-deep water and trotted up the bank, shaking his mane as he climbed up.

"Yes!" I cheered. "You did it!"

For a second, I wouldn't have cared if Charm ran out or refused a jump after that. He'd conquered his fear of water and he would be more confident every time we did cross-country and made it through a creek.

"Ready to finish this?" I asked. I gave him an extra inch of rein. "Let's go!"

Charm started to canter and his hooves pounded the dirt as we swept down the straight part of the trail out of the woods. We reached the clearing and were only jumps away from the finish line.

Charm jumped two rails held by old feed buckets and bounced playfully when we landed. He was feeling proud after the creek.

We cantered up to a row of old tires and Charm jumped them, hitting the ground inches away from the obstacle.

"Two more," I said. "Then we're done!"

The reins had worked up a white foam against Charm's sweaty neck. His breathing was getting heavier, but he didn't slow for a second. Charm jumped a tall hedge and didn't come close to touching the leaves below.

"Almost there," I told him.

All that separated us from the YENT was the stone wall. Charm asked for more rein and I let him into a faster canter, knowing he needed a boost to get over the final jump. I started counting it down.

Three.

The last jump before the YENT.

Two.

A summer at home, or at camp.

One.

Charm rocked back on his haunches and pushed himself into the air. His back rounded and his forelegs snapped under his body as he arched over the wall. He landed on the other side and cantered away from the jump.

"Omigod, Charm," I said, pulling him to a trot and then a walk. "You were perfect!"

I hopped off his back and hurried to loosen his girth. His nostrils flared pink and his chest heaved. But he shook out his mane—he knew he'd been amazing.

"I love you so much," I said. I hugged his neck and walked him over to Mr. Conner.

"Fantastic, Sasha," Mr. Conner said. He knelt down and ran his hands over Charm's legs. "Let's get him back to the stable and Mike will check all his vitals. You can run back to Winchester to change for your interview with Mr. Nicholson."

"Okay," I said. "Thanks."

Mr. Conner went back to the course and I smiled when I saw Eric.

"Mr. Conner told all of us not to bother the riders before their interviews," Eric said.

"You're not bothering me," I said. "But I do have to take Charm back to the stable."

Eric looked at Charm. "Yeah. He looks tired, but he was amazing. You guys killed it!"

That made me feel a little less exhausted. "Thanks. Really."

"It's true. I'd walk you to the stable, but Mr. Conner told me to stay here in case he needs help."

"Okay," I said. "I'll meet you at the Sweet Shoppe."

I started to walk away, then realized that my parents *and* Eric would want to hang out with me after the interview.

"Eric?" I said. "I forgot—my parents will be there after and . . . I don't want to make you uncomfortable."

"Why would I be uncomfortable?" Eric asked.

"Because you'd have to meet them and I don't want you to feel pressured or anything. If you want, I'll text you when we're done or something."

"They're your parents," Eric said. "I *want* to meet them."

"Really?"

"Really. See you at the Sweet Shoppe?"

We smiled at each other, then I turned Charm and led him to the stable. I shook my head—maybe it was just a misunderstanding—or even bad advice. But I couldn't help thinking that Jacob had lied to me on purpose.

A couple of hours later, Heather, Callie, Jasmine, and I were sitting outside Mr. Conner's office, showered, changed, and waiting for him to call our names. No one had said a word about cross-country. It was our little secret about how we'd done.

"Jasmine," Mr. Conner said, walking up to us. "Mr. Nicholson is ready for you now."

She walked into Mr. Conner's office and closed the door. I stared ahead, not able to look at anyone. Fainting seemed like a definite possibility. Beside me Callie was all business in black pants and a gray and white striped shirt.

A few minutes later the door opened and a smiling Jasmine emerged. She flounced by us without a word and disappeared down the aisle. Heather was called in next.

Callie leaned her head against the wall behind her and looked at me. "I'm exhausted."

"Me too. But I don't think it was just the riding. We've been stressing about this for months and now it's over."

"Except for that," Callie said, tipping her head in the direction of Mr. Conner's office.

"True, but it'll only take a few minutes. And we are sparkling conversationalists," I said, laughing.

"Why yes," Callie said. "We are."

We cracked up, then stopped laughing when the door opened and Heather walked out. She nodded at me and kept walking.

"You'll be fine," Callie whispered.

I stood and rubbed my sweaty hands on my gray and pink striped skirt. I walked into the office and sat across from Mr. Nicholson, who was seated behind Mr. Conner's desk.

"Hi, Sasha," Mr. Nicholson said. "Thanks for talking with me for a few minutes."

"Thank you for watching me ride," I said, my voice shaky.

Mr. Nicholson glanced at a file, then took off his rimless glasses and placed them on the table. "You did a respectable job today. I'm most impressed with your connection to Charm. The work you did at the creek was impressive."

"That's where you were?" I blurted out.

Mr. Nicholson chuckled. "Yes. Mr. Conner told me what areas each of you were struggling with. I wanted to watch you and Charm at the creek to see how you handled whatever situation arose."

"I've been working with him for weeks on that," I said. "I'm just glad he went through it."

"Your hard work was evident, Sasha. Charm trusted you to get him through the water."

"Thank you."

"Now, I've got a few questions for you." Mr. Nicholson sat back in his chair. "Why do you want to ride for the Youth Equestrian National Team?"

"It's all I've ever wanted to do," I said. "I wasn't sure how I'd get there when I lived in Union and rode at Briar Creek. I knew I needed to come to a place like Canterwood, but I was scared to leave home."

Mr. Nicholson nodded.

"But I if I wanted the best shot at becoming a professional equestrian, leaving home was necessary. I came to Canterwood at the beginning of the school year and I don't regret that decision. I'm growing every day as a rider and I know I'd do that on the YENT as well."

Mr. Nicholson folded his hands. His face gave away nothing. "What specific skills would you bring to the team?"

I met his eyes. "I don't have as much formal training as the other riders, but I work hard. I'm strongest in cross-country and am practicing dressage. I'll work hard every day that I'm on the team."

"And what are your riding goals for your eighth-grade year?" Mr. Nicholson asked. He slid a manila file in front of him.

"I want to become a more well-rounded rider," I said. "I need to work more on dressage. And honestly, I'm still trying to find the balance between obsessing about riding and focusing on other things too."

Mr. Nicholson smiled. "If you figure that out anytime soon, please let me know."

"Okay," I promised. "I will."

"Sasha, that's about it. Thank you for answering my questions and for working so hard. I will be phoning Mr. Conner tomorrow with my decision. I am giving every rider serious thought."

"Thank you, sir," I said. We both stood and I shook his hand. I left the office and let out a giant sigh when I saw Callie waiting on the bench.

"He's so nice!" I said. "You're going to do great."

Callie stood and clenched her hands together. "Okay. Breathing."

"Seriously. Go. And I'll see you at the Sweet Shoppe in a few minutes."

I stepped out of the stable and into the sunshine. My exhaustion evaporated and I almost wanted to skip to the Sweet Shoppe. I felt lighter than I had in weeks. I stopped, opened my purse, and pulled out the lip gloss I'd bought last week and had saved for today. I twisted open the top and pulled out the wand. Lip Sparkler in cotton candy clouds—yum! I applied some and put it back in my purse. It was the perfect "Happy Summer!" treat.

I pulled the door to the Sweet Shoppe open and inhaled my favorite scents—warm cookies, frosting, and chocolate. I looked over and saw Mom, Dad, and Paige sitting together. At the back of the room, Jasmine and her parents were eating éclairs and sipping something in tiny cups.

Heather and Mr. Fox weren't here yet—I hoped everything was okay. Callie's parents had a table a few feet away and were chatting as they waited for her to finish the interview. Eric wasn't here yet—he'd probably gotten held up by Mr. Conner.

Mom, Dad, and Paige smiled at me and clapped as I sat down.

"Guys!" I said, blushing. "Stop it."

"But you were so great," Paige said.

"Fine, fine!" I said, laughing and holding up my hands. "I was *awesome*. There. Happy?"

Everyone laughed.

"Not quite," Dad said. "Not until you have a treat for your special day."

He caught someone's eye at the counter and a barista walked over. She gave everyone a Coke in a glass bottle—so cool—and passed out plates.

"What did you order?" I asked.

Mom shook her head. "Just wait a sec."

Two baristas came over, carrying a giant tray. They lowered it onto the middle of the table. I gasped when I looked at it. It was a *huge* square chocolate cake with white frosting. But in the center, a girl in green and gold jumped a gorgeous chestnut horse over a vertical. *Congrats Sasha & Charm!* was written in hot pink icing along the top of the cake.

"Mom! Dad!" I said. "I don't even know if I made the team."

Dad reached over and put his hand on top of mine. "It's not about the team, sweetie. It's about you working hard all year to get to this point. We're so proud of everything you've done."

"Thanks," I said, trying not to get all sniffly. "It's perfect."

Dad stood and walked up to Mr. Harper, holding out his camera. "Would you mind?"

"Not at all," Mr. Harper said. He came over and held the camera to his eye. Paige slung her arm across my shoulders and Mom and Dad leaned in. Mr. Harper snapped a couple of shots.

"Congratulations on a great year, Sasha," he said. "I know Callie's proud to have you as her friend."

"I feel the same about her," I said. "Thanks."

I texted Eric once I sat down.

R u coming? Got cake.

Dad got a knife and cut the cake. He handed me the first piece and I dug into it. Mmmm. I checked my phone, but Eric still hadn't texted back. We were about to have a second piece—special occasion, hello!—when Callie walked in. She motioned for me to come over.

"Be right back," I said, getting up. I walked over to Callie and she pulled me beside the counter. "What's wrong? Did something happen at your interview?"

Callie shook her head. "No, that went great. It was Mr. Fox and Mr. Conner."

"What?"

"When I left my interview, I heard two people arguing in the side aisle. Mr. Fox told Mr. Conner that he didn't think Heather had been prepared enough for the YENT tryout and he wanted to know exactly how many hours she'd been riding every day."

"Omigod. What did Mr. Conner say?"

"He was maaad. He told Mr. Fox that Heather rode more than most students and she was one of the hardest-working riders on the team. He basically said that Mr. Fox was pressuring Heather too much and it wasn't going to help her become a better rider."

"Whoa. I bet Mr. Fox loved that."

Callie shook her head. "I left before I got caught. But I'm glad Mr. Conner stood up for her. Mr. Fox did say he was going back to his hotel, so I think Heather will be fine."

The Sweet Shoppe door opened and Jacob walked over.

"Hey," he said to Callie and me.

"Hi," I said. "You better celebrate with Callie. She's sooo already a YENT member."

"I know she is," Jacob said. "I'm thinking cake."

Callie and Jacob went to sit with Mr. and Mrs. Harper and I returned to my table. I watched them out of the corner of my eye and saw the relief on Callie's face that Jacob was finally acting like his old self.

The door opened again and Heather walked in. She slowed as she walked past our table, but didn't look at us.

"Heather?" I called.

She stopped and turned back, folding her arms. "What?"

"We have tons of cake if you want some."

There was a hint of a smile. "Sure," she said. "While I wait for *my* friends."

She ate a piece of cake and Mom asked her questions about her ride. The more Mom asked, the easier it was to get Heather to talk.

After Dad took cake to the Harpers and the Kings (eww), the parents grouped together and stood in front of us.

"As much as we'd like to think that you want to hang out with the old people all night," Mrs. Harper said. "We know better. We're going back to our hotel now, just in case you kids want to—oh, I don't know—have some fun without us on your last night here."

"Smooth, Mom," Callie said.

Everyone, even Jasmine, smiled at that.

We all said good-bye to our parents and they left the shop.

"I love my parents," I said. "I really do."

"But . . . ," Paige prompted, grinning.

"But she sooo wanted to hang out with her friends tonight!" Callie finished.

We laughed. "What should we do?" Paige asked.

"Definitely pizza," Jacob said. "Anyone else?"

"Definitely," I said.

I looked up when Eric came inside. He walked over to our table and sat beside me.

"Sorry I'm late," he said. "Mr. Conner asked me to help with a chart and I got stuck at the stable. Did I miss your parents?"

"Yeah," I said. "But it's okay. You'll meet them another time."

I couldn't stop smiling, looking around at all of my teammates and friends. Tonight wasn't about the YENT. It was a celebration of making it through one of the craziest school years ever. And that deserved some pepperoni pizza.

31

SLEEP WELL!

WHEN PAIGE AND I LEFT FOR THE NEW PIZZA place on campus—The Slice—we couldn't stop giggling. It felt like summer and we'd dressed in T-shirts, jeans, and flip-flops.

"Why are we laughing again?" I asked, trying to breathe.

Paige shook her head. "We're laughing at nothing. It's called 'delirium.' We're so tired because we just finished finals. But we're also insanely excited because they're *over*."

"Sooo over!"

I pulled open the door and inhaled scents of melted cheese and yummy sauce. The shop was adorable with red and white checkered table cloths and old-fashioned lanterns that gave off a warm glow. Behind the giant white counter, a man in a white apron tossed dough high in the air, then spun it on his fingers. Troy, Andy, Ben, and Nicole were already sitting at the biggest table in the center of the room.

Paige and I grabbed seats by Nicole.

"Pizza was the *perfect* idea for tonight," Nicole said. "We all had to hang out one more time before summer. But how lame that Canterwood didn't open a pizza place until the last week of school."

"Totally," I said. "And, plus, I'm kind of starving."

Heather, Julia, and Alison came in and snagged three chairs at the end of the table. They started whispering and Heather looked around, probably checking to see if her BFF Jas was here yet.

Eric walked in and sat across from me. "We're doing dessert again tonight, right?" he asked.

"Do you know me at all?" I asked. "Of course!"

Callie and Jacob stepped inside, holding hands and laughing. Jacob whispered something in Callie's ear when he pulled out a chair for her.

Everyone said hi to each other and then we all started talking at once. The table quieted, though, when Jasmine and the Belles walked in. The girls walked to the opposite end of the table from the Trio and sat down. I watched them, waiting for them to glare or make a joke about what losers we were and why they'd really come to eat with us. But they only started talking to each other and ignored the rest of us. Maybe everyone was really here just to have fun for once.

Callie caught my eye and pointed to the bathroom. Eric was talking to Nicole about how he worked Luna over cavaletti yesterday, so I just motioned to him that I'd be right back. Callie and I walked to the bathroom together and the second the door shut behind us, Callie turned to me, her eyes wide.

"Jacob apologized for being weird," she said. "Finally!"

"Really? That's great! Did he say what was wrong?"

"He wasn't superspecific, but he said there had been something going on with a friend. But he's over it now."

"See?" I asked. "Told you it was nothing you did."

Callie nodded. "I'm so relieved. I bet it was his roommate. I think they were having a fight or something."

"I'm so glad that's over," I said. "Now you're going to have a great time tonight."

We linked arms and walked out of the bathroom. Someone had ordered the pizzas while we'd been gone and minutes later, we were stuffing our faces with cheesy goodness.

"What're you doing this summer?" Eric asked Julia.

She wiped her mouth with a napkin. "Staying home. Trying to convince my parents to let me at least school Trix."

"Same here," Alison said. "I don't want to spend all summer at the movies."

"You?" Nicole asked Eric.

"Riding at my hometown stable," Eric said. "My old instructor said I could help break and train a new horse."

"Really?" Troy asked. "That's cool."

"Paige," I said. "What about *you*?"

Paige picked a green pepper off her pizza. "Um, just working. And hanging out in the city."

"Paige." I folded my arms and looked at her. I knew Paige would never want me to mention that she'd also be on the lookout for Ryan.

Paige blushed, playing with her hair. "What?"

"C'mon. Don't be modest."

Paige took a breath. "Okay, okay. I'm filming *Teen Cuisine* episodes this summer."

"And you didn't want to talk about it because . . . ?" Troy asked.

Paige took a sip of soda. "Because I don't want everyone to think I'm a snob."

"*No* one would think that, ever," Callie said. "We love hearing about *TC*."

"Really?" Paige sat up a little straighter.

"What happens on set?" Nicole asked.

As Paige talked, I noticed that even Jasmine and the Belles leaned over to listen.

We ate and chatted for more than an hour before people started to leave. Soon, Nicole, Troy, Andy, and Ben were gone. The Belles and Jasmine got up and headed for the door. Violet, pausing, turned around and looked at us. Her eyes shifted from Heather, to Callie, to me.

"None of you have a chance at the YENT," Violet said with a smile. "We've been coaching Jasmine for weeks. She's the only Canterwood rider who will make it, wait and see."

"Then you'll sleep well tonight," Heather said.

Violet locked eyes with Heather, almost as if she was going to argue. But she turned and walked out with the other girls trailing behind her.

"And with that, I'm out of here," Heather said, standing. "Later." Alison and Julia left with her.

I swirled my spoon in my bowl, catching any last remnants of hot fudge from my sundae. "I'm ready to go too. Now I just want to go to sleep so tomorrow gets here."

"Agreed," Callie said.

Paige, Eric, Callie, Jacob, and I left the restaurant. We walked together until Paige and I reached the fork in the sidewalk where we needed to split up.

"Fingers crossed about tomorrow," I said, hugging Callie.

"You too," she said. "I really, really believe we made it."

Eric and Jacob stared at each other for a second, but didn't say anything.

"Talk to you tomorrow," Eric said, squeezing my hand and giving me a quick kiss. He turned to Paige. "And thanks for distracting Sasha tonight—I know you'll be doing that."

"Anytime," Paige said. "I've got the DVDs ready."

Paige and I walked toward Winchester and I thought about how great tonight had been. Everyone—minus the Belles—was getting along. I had my BFF back and we both had amazing boyfriends. Paige was about to have a fab summer as a TV star and Jacob and I were even kind of friends again. My last night at Canterwood couldn't have been better.

32

A YES OR A NO?

LAST NIGHT HAD BEEN THE OPPOSITE OF what I'd expected. Instead of lying awake all night, I'd fallen asleep right away. Now all I could do was stare at my phone, willing Mr. Conner to call with news.

"Aren't you glad you didn't wake up any earlier?" Paige asked. "'Cause you've been watching that phone for two hours."

"I know," I said. "But I can't miss this call."

Paige kept packing her shoes into her suitcase. "But guess what? You don't have to watch a phone to make it ring. You should do something to distract yourself."

I nodded and got up off my bed, tossing my phone on the comforter and looking at its dark screen one last time. "You're right. I really do need to check to be sure I've got everything. Mom and Dad will be here—"

Riiinngg!

"Omigodomigod!" I dashed across the carpet and grabbed my phone, almost dropping it.

"Hello?" I answered, barely able to get out the word.

"Hi, Sasha. It's Mr. Conner. Mr. Nicholson has informed me of his decision. I need to see you in my office now, all right?"

"Okay. Yes. Okay. Thank you."

I closed the phone and clutched it, staring at Paige. "This is it. I'm either on the YENT or I'm not."

I started to sit down, but Paige reached over and pulled me up. "Go. Right now. You've been waiting for this answer for months. Sasha, either way, you did your best and you know it. Go get your answer."

I nodded, taking a deep breath. "You're right. Okay. I need to know. Going now."

I walked out of Winchester, forcing myself not to take the long way. But I wished the walk took longer than five minutes. Being in limbo—*did I make it or not?*—was almost easier than this walk to his office. In minutes, I'd have an answer. No gray area. A yes or a no.

Heather and Callie were standing outside Mr. Conner's closed door, just staring at it.

"I can't go in," Callie whispered. "I'm too scared."

Heather nodded, not even trying to fake nonchalance.

"I almost don't want to know," I said.

The three of us stood there, waiting for someone to make a move.

"Oh, go in already, losers," said a voice behind us. Jasmine pushed her way between Callie and me and knocked on the door.

"Come in," Mr. Conner called.

Jasmine opened his door and walked into the office, taking a seat.

Barely breathing, I sat next to Callie.

"Thanks for coming," Mr. Conner said. "I called you in as soon as I spoke with Mr. Nicholson. He knew you were all eager to hear his decision."

No one spoke. We couldn't.

Mr. Conner looked at each of us. "I don't want to drag this out, but I do want to tell you how proud I am. You're each talented and hardworking riders and without those qualities, you never would have made it this far. The YENT can only take so many riders, but no matter what, you all should be proud of yourselves."

Five minutes ago, I hadn't wanted to hear the decision. Now I was dying. *Spill it already!*

"I want to remind you that any rider who is chosen

must attend summer training camp," Mr. Conner said. "It will be intense and demanding—much more than our midwinter break clinic."

Say. It. Now.

"I'm going to announce Mr. Nicholson's decision," Mr. Conner said. "Starting with Heather."

She swallowed when he said her name. I crossed my fingers for her—something I never would have done last fall. But I didn't want to see her lose Aristocrat.

"Heather," Mr. Conner said. "You've made the team."

Heather covered her mouth with her hand. "Omigod—um. Omigod! Wow."

"Congrats!" Callie said.

"That's awesome," I said. "Congratulations."

Heather nodded at us. Jasmine didn't even look in Heather's direction. Color came back to Heather's face and I knew the relief wasn't just about making the team. She'd secured her future at Canterwood and she'd kept Aristocrat.

"Jasmine," Mr. Conner said. "You'll also be joining Heather on the team."

Jas just smiled and nodded as if she'd known all along.

Callie and I looked at each other. We'd both known she'd make it.

Mr. Conner's eyes settled on me. *Don't cry, don't cry, don't cry,* I repeated to myself.

"Sasha," Mr. Conner said. "Congratulations. You're a member of the YENT."

"I knew it!" Callie squealed. She hugged me and I started laughing, trying not to cry.

"I made it!" I said. "I really made the YENT. No. Way."

I flopped back into my chair. Everything Charm and I had worked for had happened. We were *both* members of the Youth Equestrian National Team. I wanted to tell Eric, Paige, Mom, and Dad right now!

Then I remembered Callie. I grabbed her hand and looked expectantly at Mr. Conner, waiting for him to say her name. Mr. Conner looked down at his desk and then back up at Callie.

"Callie," Mr. Conner said, pausing. "Your rides were excellent and Mr. Nicholson was impressed."

I looked over at Callie, smiling at her.

Mr. Conner shook his head. "But I'm sorry. You did not make the team."

What?!

Oh.

My.

God.

Callie just stared at Mr. Conner. She didn't move—not even a blink. Her hand went limp in mine.

"I'm sorry, Callie," Mr. Conner said. "Mr. Nicholson put a lot of thought into his decision and he ultimately decided that you just weren't ready. He'll be looking to add a rider or two in the fall and he wants to watch you test again."

Callie finally nodded. "Okay. Thanks." Her voice was barely above a whisper.

Mr. Conner looked at Callie—he knew she wasn't okay.

"You may leave now," Mr. Conner said. "Thank you for working hard this year and I hope you have a good summer. If any of you"—he looked at Callie—"need to talk about this, please call or e-mail me."

We got up and shuffled out of his office. Jasmine walked away, not even bothering to manage a "sorry" to Callie.

Callie sat on the bench outside of Mr. Conner's office. Heather and I sat on either side of her. Callie took a deep breath.

"Callie," I said. "I'm so sorry. Mr. Nicholson made a huge mistake."

Heather leaned forward so she could look at Callie and

see me. "You did the best you could," Heather said. "You practiced as hard as all of us."

"But I didn't," Callie said, her voice calm. "That's why I'm not losing it right now. I didn't work hard—not even close."

Heather's eyes connected with mine for a second.

"What are you talking about?" Heather asked. "That's so not true."

I shook my head. "You worked *hard*."

"I did practice, but not like I needed to," Callie said. "I knew for months about tryouts and I let myself get distracted by other things."

Heather, sighing, stood up. Her face was flushed and she paused before looking at Callie. "You're allowed to have a life, you know," she said. "Not everything has to be about riding. And take that from someone who's just figuring it out."

Heather walked away, leaving Callie and me alone. Callie and I sat in silence for a few minutes before Callie turned to me.

"I got too caught up in Jacob," Callie said. "And I was afraid that would happen from the second I started to like him."

I was quiet, knowing Callie needed to get it out.

"I didn't work hard enough," Callie said. "I just didn't."

I shifted on the wooden bench, turning sideways to look at her. "You don't have be so calm. It's okay to be upset."

Callie shrugged. "But I did this. I chose to be late to practice and I made the decisions not to ride more on weekends. I can't blame Mr. Nicholson for not picking me when I didn't deserve a spot on the team."

"I think you're being too hard on yourself. Heather was right, which is kind of weird but true. We're all learning how to juggle things. It doesn't make you any less dedicated of a rider if you want to hang out with your boyfriend instead of riding every minute of every day."

"But I used to be so focused," Callie said. She ran her fingers through her hair. "The old Callie would break up with Jacob right now, ride all summer, and ensure she got a spot on the YENT this fall. But I'm still crazy about Jacob and I don't want to give him up."

"You shouldn't," I said. "I love that you're so happy with him. You deserve to be happy."

Callie smiled. "Thanks. And I do want to figure out how to handle things so I can make the YENT, but riding isn't the only thing in my life anymore."

"You'll make it," I promised. "And you know I'm here for you in the meantime."

"I know. We'll probably see more of each other on iChat than we have in the past couple of weeks."

We hugged and Callie checked the time on her phone. "I've got to go finish packing before my parents get here."

"Yeah, me too." I shook my head. "Our last day on campus as seventh graders. Wow."

Callie laughed. "There were a few times this year that I didn't think we'd see eighth grade."

"No kidding. For a while, I wasn't sure if we'd survive Heather, Jas, or the Belles."

We laughed and Callie stood up. "You have to update me every day from YENT camp," Callie said. "Or we won't be friends anymore."

I crossed my heart with a Princesses Rule–tipped finger. "Promise. You'll be sick of my updates."

We hugged again and Callie walked away. When she was gone, I stood in the aisle, processing everything that had happened. Callie was going to be okay—she had Jacob. And me. She'd make the team in the fall.

And I'd *already* made it. I was going to YENT camp!

I hurried down the aisle, almost running into Julia and Alison.

"We heard from Heather," Alison said. "Congratulations."

Julia nodded slowly. "Yeah. I'm glad you made it."

"Thanks," I said. "And I hope things work out for you this summer so you'll be riding in the fall."

The girls nodded.

"We will be," Alison said. "You'll see."

I had no idea what that meant, but I didn't doubt it for a second.

They walked away and I left the stable, barely able to stand not being able to tell someone right now. Paige had been there for me since the first day of school and she deserved to hear the news first. Then, I'd go find Eric. This time, the distance between the stable and Winchester never felt so long.

33

CONFESSION

"PAAAAIIGGE!" I CALLED, PUSHING OPEN OUR dorm room door. "Guess what?"

"You made it!" Paige squealed, throwing a handful of confetti in the air. Pink, purple, and silver bits of paper rained down on me and fell at my feet.

"Did someone already tell you?" I asked.

Paige grinned. "I just knew. You don't ride like Sasha Silver and not make the YENT."

I mock-rolled my eyes. "Puh-lease."

"You won't roll your eyes after you see this," Paige said. She reached behind a big box on her desk and presented a cupcake with a candle stuck in the middle. The cupcake's pink frosting was swirled into a tip. Clear, diamondlike sprinkles made the icing glitter.

"Paige! It's gorgeous. You so didn't have to do that."

Paige handed me the cupcake and took one for herself. "I wanted to. I'm just mad that Livvie wouldn't let me light the candle in here."

I licked at the frosting. "Tell the truth."

"What?" Paige blinked innocently.

"Livvie wouldn't let you give a lighted cupcake to *me*. She thought I'd start a fire somehow."

Paige shrugged. "That might have been true."

We giggled and ate our delicious victory cupcakes.

"YENT camp is going to be tough, huh?" Paige asked.

I tossed my cupcake paper in the trash. "For sure. Mr. Conner said it would be harder than the clinic."

"You're going to need a break after that," Paige said. "Sooo . . . I was thinking that you could come stay with me for a couple of weeks this summer after YENT camp. We could hang out in the city *and* you could come to the *Teen Cuisine* set."

"Really?! I'd *love* that! We'd have so much fun!"

Paige smiled. "I know. I'm already planning lots of stuff for us to do."

"This is going to be the best summer ever," I said.

"For sure!" Paige said. She looked at the wall clock and her eyes widened. "My parents will be here in fifteen minutes."

While she finished packing, I grabbed my phone and texted Eric. *Meet me @ crtyrd now?*

BRT.

"Be back in a few minutes," I told Paige.

I walked to the courtyard, unable to stop smiling. The campus had never looked so gorgeous—the grass surrounding the courtyard was green and lush, the sunlight bounced off the water fountains, and the pink, red, yellow, and purple tulips that had been closed for weeks had opened, splashing color everywhere.

But the best sight was Eric waiting by the fountain. He turned, and when he saw me, he knew. I ran up to him and threw my arms around him.

"I knew you'd make it," he said, lifting me off my feet and swinging me around. "I'm so happy for you!"

"I'm pretty happy too," I said, catching my breath as he lowered me to the ground. "I really made it."

"I never doubted it," Eric said. "This is the best reason ever for you to leave the advanced team. I'm so proud of you, Sash."

Eric took my hand and we sat at the edge of the fountain. "What about everyone else?" he asked. "Who made it?"

I sighed, still feeling sad for Callie. "Heather and Jasmine made it. Callie didn't."

Eric slumped a little. "Oh, wow. Poor Callie. That's awful. I know how much she wanted it."

"She was upset, but she knows what she has to do to make it this fall. We're going to chat and text all summer and I think she'll want it even more after she hears about YENT camp."

"That's right," Eric said. "YENT camp. You'll become even more of a superstar rider this summer."

I smiled. "And my boyfriend's going to become a famous horse trainer."

"We're both going to have great summers," he said. "And we'll have to iChat a lot—I want to see you."

"Me too."

Eric's phone rang and he pulled it out of his pocket. "Hey, Mom. Okay. Sure. See you in a minute."

Eric closed his phone and turned to me. "They're here to pick me up."

We stood. "Have an amazing summer," I said in Eric's ear as he wrapped me in a hug.

"You too, Sash."

Eric leaned in to give me one last kiss and squeezed my hand. "Text you later."

I watched him walk away, feeling a million emotions about Eric and YENT camp. I'd miss Eric, but I knew we'd talk every day. YENT camp would be intense and I was nervous that I wouldn't be ready for it. But being scared about going to YENT camp was better than being comfortable at Briar Creek all summer.

I reached for my phone to see if Mom and Dad were almost here. I was *dying* to tell them.

"Sasha," someone called.

I looked up and saw Jacob walking toward me. One of his black Chucks was untied and his T-shirt was wrinkled. His green eyes looked worried.

"You heard about Callie," I said. "I'm so sorry. She's going to be okay though."

Jacob stopped in front of me. "I know. I feel awful that she didn't make it."

"We'll be there for her," I said. "And she's so happy to have you—"

"Sasha, stop." Jacob shook his head. "This isn't about Callie."

"What?"

Jacob's eyes locked on mine.

"What?" I looked at him, confused. "Just tell me."

He took a deep breath. "Sasha, I got the e-mail you wrote me. I got it a few weeks ago. I tried to forget about it, I really did."

The e-mail.

The e-mail I'd sent to Jacob before my kiss with Eric, where I'd confessed that I still liked him and wondered if we could try again. He'd never responded, so I thought it had been lost in cyberspace until Violet taunted me that she had a copy. She'd sent Jacob the intercepted e-mail.

I was not hearing this. "Don't—" I started to say, but Jacob stepped closer.

"I like Callie," he said, his eyes searching my face. "But—"

"But what?" I asked, barely able to get enough breath to ask.

The scared look on Jacob's face vanished. "I can't stop thinking about you."

All I could do was stare at him. This had to be a dream. Jacob was *not* saying this. Not now. The rainbow of tulips swirled around us.

"Callie's a great girl," Jacob said. "And I care about her. But I don't think about her the way I think about you. I messed up, Sasha. I didn't see it before . . . but now I do."

After everything that had happened—Jacob breaking up with me, liking Eric, losing Callie, almost messing things up with Eric and getting Callie back—now Jacob was confessing that he wanted me back? After the worst couple of months ever, everything had finally fallen into place. Things between Eric and me were *perfect*. Callie—I mean, it had taken forever for us to become friends again. If she found out—

"Sasha?" Jacob asked. He reached out to me, but I shook my head. Tears made Jacob blurry.

"I can't deal with this right now," I choked out. I backed away a couple of steps and then turned and did the only thing I could think to do: I spun around and ran out of the courtyard, leaving Jacob staring after me.

ABOUT THE AUTHOR

Twenty-two-year-old Jessica Burkhart is a writer from New York City. Like Sasha, she's crazy about horses, lip gloss, and all things pink and sparkly. Before she started writing, Jess was an equestrian and had a horse like Charm. To watch Jess's vlogs and read her blog, visit www.jessicaburkhart.com.

www.LiPSMACKER.com
LiP SMACKER®
LOUNGE
Check out hot new movies and music
Post your favorite pictures
Create a colorful, new avatar
Quiz yourself and your friends
Tell us what you think
Share your creativity
Show off your Lip Smacker collection
Explore ways to start a collection
Download popular video links
Find out the latest celebrity buzz
Express your favorite flavor
www.lipsmacker.com ©2009 Bonne Bell, Inc.®

metimes a girl just needs a good book.

Lauren Barnholdt understands.

And coming September 2009:

DORK diaries

Tales from a NOT-SO-Fabulous Life

She's a self-proclaimed dork. She has the coolest pen ever. She keeps a top-secret diary.
Read it if you dare.

By Rachel Renee Russell

From Aladdin
Published by Simon & Schuster